THE LEGACY SERIES

their circumstances, by the strictures of society, by their own damn selves, staring down dreams deferred. 'Would they be stuck in the dim hallway forever?' Nevins refuses pat, easy answers. 'But I want to know what they're saying.' Readers of this wide-ranging, far-reaching collection will keep turning pages, spurred on by that wanting, too."

—Sara Lippmann
author of *Lech* and *Jerks*

THE COMMISSION OF INQUIRY — STORIES

PATRICK NEVINS

CORNERSTONE PRESS
UNIVERSITY OF WISCONSIN-STEVENS POINT

Cornerstone Press, Stevens Point, Wisconsin 54481
Copyright © 2024 Patrick Nevins
www.uwsp.edu/cornerstone

Printed in the United States of America by
Point Print and Design Studio, Stevens Point, Wisconsin

Library of Congress Control Number: 2024930747
ISBN: 978-1-960329-19-6

This is a work of fiction. Names, characters, businesses, places, events, and incidents are either the products of the author's imagination or used in a fictitious manner. Any resemblance to actual persons, living or dead, or actual events is purely coincidental.

Cornerstone Press titles are produced in courses and internships offered by the Department of English at the University of Wisconsin–Stevens Point.

DIRECTOR & PUBLISHER
Dr. Ross K. Tangedal

EXECUTIVE EDITORS
Jeff Snowbarger, Freesia McKee

EDITORIAL DIRECTOR
Ellie Atkinson

SENIOR EDITORS
Brett Hill, Grace Dahl

PRESS STAFF
Madalyn Carpenter, Carolyn Czerwinski, Alex Diaz, Sophie McPherson, Kylie Newton, Eva Nielsen, Josh Paulson, Natalie Reiter, Lauren Rudesill, Katie Schimke, Ava Willett

For Lucy and Will

ALSO BY PATRICK NEVINS:

Man in a Cage

STORIES

MY FATHER AND RAY GUN

My paternal grandfather was there when Reagan toured the GE plant where he ran the canteen. Reagan held the men in a trance while he painted a picture of the federal government as a bloated monster eating away the men's liberty. No man, including my grandfather, would forget him. Probably for the rest of their lives, and certainly not a few years later when Reagan endorsed Goldwater. My grandfather voted for LBJ anyway, since he was going to end Vietnam. He died before the war ended.

My father heard the story about Reagan's speech at the GE plant, and it must've stuck with him. He knew Reagan as the governor of California next, though we were in a flyover state, not the Golden State. He went to the polls for him in '80 and '84, certain that he would make America great again.

We were far from Washington, but I came to know the president through harDCore eyes. Hey, Hey, Hey, Hey, Heyyyyy, Ronnie! When I wore a t-shirt of a monstrously headed Ronnie running a lawnmower over a crowd, my father made me throw it in the trash.

I recovered the shirt from the trash that night and hand-washed it in the basement sink, though I couldn't get out a spaghetti stain on one corner of the image; it looked like the people's blood. I hid the shirt under a worn-out Oxford or sweater when I went to shows.

Somewhere in the last thirty years, I lost the shirt. An Internet search shows that I can get a "Mowing Down the People Classic '80s Punk T-Shirt" for $19.99, though I'm not sure what my motivation would be for such a purchase. I'm not sure what my motivation was then. I like to think that I wanted to be an ally to the people under that lawnmower: the poor, the ghettoized, the victims of AIDS. What about their liberty? I might've asked my father. But it might be closer to the truth that I was swept up in punk and its requisite stances. Or maybe just its requisite impoliteness; I must've wanted to piss my father off. I didn't yet know the story about his father and Reagan at the GE plant, though I doubt it would've made any difference. He told me about it only a few years ago. I remembered the shirt, and I think he did, too. There's no word for what we exchanged in that moment, for the uneasy blend of resentment and resignation, stirred up by our memories of a decades-old argument. Since there were no words for what we were feeling, there were no words to say. I laughed, and he smiled sympathetically and asked what was funny. Nothing, I said, I'm just trying to remember where I left something.

ENOS

Cameroon

The chimp came to life at dawn. As a hazy glow filled the canopy, he roused himself in his nest of mangrove leaves and searched the nearby trees for his mother. She was a short distance away, nursing his infant sister, whom he adored. Whenever he gently tickled her chin, she would turn her eyes toward him; they were shimmering black orbs circled in white. Their mother's eyes. He had not seen any other chimps with eyes like theirs.

Having sighted his family, the chimp returned his attention to his own nest. He had woven its wide leaves into a thick bed, smoothed out the lumps, and pressed the little mattress into a crook in a mangrove tree so that it made a bowl into which he had curled up as yesterday's light faded. It was his best work yet. He was of the age that he no longer shared his mother's nest, but he was many seasons from when he would test himself against the mature males of his family's group. It was a critical period in which he was learning the art of nest-making and ant-catching and practicing his displays of power and virility. As it was, the mature chimps paid him little attention; he was a tawny-muzzled youth who built his nests close to his mother and infant sister. He still nursed.

At midday, on the forest floor, the chimp rocked on his rump, watching his sister nurse and waiting his turn. It was at precisely this moment that the trouble began. Some hidden threat set the mature males to screaming. Their panic was more fevered than any outburst the chimp had ever witnessed over elephant herds or rogue male chimps. It pressed against his eardrums, and the first tremors of panic pounded in his heart. Then a terrible sound echoed through the forest, breaking it apart. The mature males scattered, as if each were trying to grab hold of his piece of the breaking-apart forest. The mothers struggled to gather their young. The chimp turned to his mother and a second forest-breaking crack sounded; his mother dropped like a mango falling from a tree. His sister wailed; the whites of her eyes enlarged (the image was imprinted on the chimp). Then she sprang from their mother's side and into nearby foliage. The chimp turned around to see what had frightened her. A strange, white ape grabbed the chimp by the arm and forced him into a thing for which he had no concept: a cage.

Miami Rare Bird Farm

Since the day the forest was broken, there had been many new concepts that the chimp had to construct. He built them from what they were not. *Human was not animal.* They held dominion over animals—in the forest where they slaughtered the mothers and captured the young, in the building where they sheltered and fed the chimp and the other imprisoned animals, and on the grounds where daily they gawked at and prodded them for pleasure.

The building was another thing. *Inside was not outside.* Inside was just a bigger cage! Inside, dawn and midday and evening and night were hidden from him. He would not know them except men retrieved him and the other adolescent chimps, gorillas, and monkeys from their cages each morning to walk them outside to the grounds. But the grounds were yet a larger cage! The chimp was permitted to roam freely across a grassy area divided by a canal and dotted with short trees that were totally unfit for climbing or nesting. Waterfowl decorated the canal and the banks; a menagerie of brilliantly colored birds perched in the trees; terrifying, long-legged flightless birds stomped around on thick, scaly feet; and the adolescent primates flitted about the place, some dressed in small children's clothes. But ultimately the chimp found himself barred from further movement by a wall. There appeared to be no gaps in this wall, yet visitors entered and exited from some point and walked among the animals—gawking, prodding—as it pleased them. Guests of the Miami Rare Bird Farm. AMERICA'S MOST UNUSUAL ATTRACTION. YOU WILL GET PICTURES UNBELIEV-ABLE. SEE THEM… HOLD THEM… PET THEM… FEED THEM… Animals were kept; humans were not. *Captive was not free.*

One day, the chimp was tossed an orange—something he'd never found in the forest, but which was to be had in abundance in this place. When he finished, a man approached him with a tiny sailor suit. The chimp had not been selected for this humiliation before, and he was not about to let it begin. The man took hold of one of his feet and tried to get him into the little pants, but the chimp withdrew. The man changed tactics and tried to pull the top over his head, but the chimp threw his hands up, preventing that course. A second man, who had successfully dressed a female chimp in a jumper, came over to lend a hand. This man, the chimp could tell, was going to restrain him while the first man dressed him. The chimp batted the second man's hands away and bared his teeth and screamed. The second man walked away resigned, and the first tossed the outfit aside. The chimp, having won this fight, regained his calm and took the first man's hand to be led to the grounds.

In his exploration of the wall that morning, the chimp came upon something he'd never seen before: Several birds were gathered around a man's likeness in stone—but the size of three men! The tableau of St. Francis surrounded by birds was lost upon the chimp; it just frightened him. It solidified his fear that humans held dominion over animals: the birds, the monkeys, the gorillas, and all his kind. If he were to escape from the grounds, if he were to find his way back to the forest, would there be any chimps left? Surely men could not have taken them all. They seemed interested only in the young. Surely the mature males had gathered the mothers who had survived and whatever young ones remained and put their group back together. Surely his infant sister had been adopted and was awaiting his return. Surely the forest had been made whole again.

HAM

The chimp was pulled from his cage one morning, examined, and taken to Holloman Air Force Base in New Mexico. There he was known as Number 81 of the Holloman Aerospace Medical Center Chimpanzee Colony. The colony lived in rows of cages and were not permitted sunlight or fresh air. Eighty-one preferred the Miami Rare Bird Farm to this, but he held onto the hope that should he pass the tests he was subjected to daily, he would be returned to the forest and his infant sister.

Every day the men inflicted new punishments on the chimps. It began with the box: Eighty-one was strapped into a metal box and isolated from the colony. Five minutes. Fifteen minutes. Hours. Then an even more anxiety-inducing test: A man would brush glue onto 81's muzzle, then fix a mask to him. Mask in place, 81 was bound inside an airtight "sled," which was previously shot down a track in the desert by rocket power and seconds later brought to a sudden halt, scrambling the brains of its chimpanzee passenger. The Holloman chimps were instead submerged in a pool for various periods. The chimps who had the mental resilience to withstand these terrors were submitted to a final test: the psychomotor. Eighty-one, having not been broken by the box nor the sled, was placed in a chair with a panel in front of him; the only thing restricting his movements were small plates attached to the soles of his feet, which were wired to the panel. On the panel were three squares that lit up red, white, and blue, and three corresponding levers. When one of the squares lit up, 81 had three seconds to pull the corresponding lever. He quickly found that if he didn't pull the lever in three seconds or pulled the wrong lever—ZAP! The plates delivered a painful shock to the soles of his feet. Eighty-one became very skilled at the psychomotor.

Menagerie in Flight

Notable space flights before Enos' orbit: June 11, 1948: A V-2 rocket launches Albert, a rhesus monkey, into space. His successors are also named Albert. Ironically, only Albert VI, on whose rocket one of the Air Force men had painted the words, "Alas, poor Yorick, I knew him well," returns to Earth having not shuffled off his mortal coil. November 3, 1957: On the heels of the basketball-sized satellite that tipped off the Space Race, Sputnik II carries Laika into space to die. The Soviets and their dogs! January 31, 1961: The Holloman Aerospace Medical Center chimpanzee Ham, named after the center, is launched into space—Project Mercury's test subject for Alan Shepard's flight. April 12, 1961: The Soviets surprise the United States by sending Yuri Gagarin into space; Gagarin, the first man in space, orbits Earth. May 5, 1961: Shepard becomes the first American to reach space, though he doesn't orbit; that honor will go to John Glenn on February 20 of the following year.

Enos

On November 21, 1961, Number 81 was selected as the test subject for the first American to orbit Earth. Eighty-one, now called Enos—Hebrew for "man"—ate a breakfast of Jell-O, eggs, and milk before being dressed in his tightly fitted space suit, stitched into the "couch" of his capsule, and offered some banana pellets as a distraction while a handler inserted a catheter. Enos bit the handler anyway. The capsule was closed and loaded into an Atlas 5 rocket for a scheduled three orbits. Did Enos know the five-hour wait until launch was not another test? That he was selected as the most intelligent chimp in the colony? Early on, Enos had been the most difficult of the chimps; while other apes were tethered to their handlers by one wrist, the fighting-and-biting 81 had required both of his wrists be tethered. Whether Enos regarded the five-hour wait in the rocket as another test or sensed it was the fulfillment of NASA's purpose for him (which was a test, too), he remained relaxed, all his bodily functions reading as normal. Enos achieved a calm dignity through every delay. His self-possession remained through the 6.8 g's during liftoff and 7.6 g's as the boosters were jettisoned and the sustainer engine kicked in.

Going into the first orbit, Enos started the psychomotor tests. The red, white, and blue lights flashed, and Enos quickly pulled the levers. In the first round, he performed as well as he had back at Holloman, receiving many banana pellets for correct responses and only ten shocks for incorrect ones. The shocks were a nuisance, but it was the heat that tested Enos' self-possession; a malfunction caused the capsule's temperature to creep up to 100 degrees Fahrenheit. Enos had no choice but to continue with the psychomotor. Then the psychomotor malfunctioned. Though Enos performed just as well in round two, the plates on his feet delivered thirty-five shocks; in round three, they gave him forty-one. As the psychomotor gave shock after shock, President Kennedy joked at a White House press conference that Enos had reported that "everything is perfect and working well."

The third orbit was cancelled due to the rising temperature. Enos dropped into the Atlantic, where he waited over three hours in the bobbing capsule. His self-possession remained, but it was by now a white-hot, angry thing bent on survival: When the capsule was brought onto the USS Stormes, the NASA men found that Enos had shredded his space suit and removed all the sensors and even pulled out his catheter, the still-inflated balloon be damned. The ribbons that remained of his suit were removed, and he was tethered by both wrists and applauded by the Air Force men on the aircraft carrier's deck. But Enos' celebrity would be short lived: Within three hours, John Glenn was announced as the Mercury astronaut who would be the first American to orbit Earth.

Return

Enos was returned to Holloman, where he no longer endured the terrible tests but was constantly examined. *When the men finish with me, perhaps they will return me to the forest, and I will see my sister—who's no longer an infant.* For ten months he submitted to his exams peacefully, often closing his eyes and imagining the forest, a nest of mangrove leaves, his sister's eyes. Then he began to feel unwell. The NASA men treated his dysentery with antibiotics. He could see the concern in their strange faces. But within a year of his orbits, which meant little, nothing, to him, the chimp succumbed: dreams of an unbroken forest, his mother, his sister, then peaceful release.

IT IS WHAT IT IS

The first thing Tristan did when she landed at O'Hare was order a gin-and-tonic. She marveled at its simple beauty: a rounded glass of clear, sparkling liquid pregnant with a little boulder of ice. The choice was hers to make: There was the way the G and T would bite her tongue with the pleasure-pain of scratching an itch before making its warm ripple down her body, or there was trying to unpack the reasons she'd kept her commitment to the convention so soon after Charlie.

A sip might only ignite her defenses; she would leave the drink unfinished and buy a ticket home. So, her first drink was generous. It began to dissolve the question of why. Sipping the rest of the drink finished the task. She had another.

In the cab ride to the convention hotel, she told herself that would be it. There was dinner tonight with the *Kids' Television Network* gang, from which she could politely duck out early. Tomorrow she was putting in a few hours at the *KTN* booth on the convention floor, a geek's paradise of comics and TV and movies—hardly a place for triggers. Saturday morning was the *KTN* panel; the only thing she'd be jonesing for then is coffee. Then it was back home. Simple.

The convention was already at full-tilt when Tristan reached check-in. She went unrecognized by the hordes of teenagers who'd descended on downtown Chicago to salivate over, what? Comic book artists and minor *Star Wars* actors?

There existed a class of geeks who would geek over her, or else why had she been asked to come? She tried to imagine them: men in their forties (it had been—my God!—thirty years!) who would blush and ask for a picture. And why not? She'd been the star of *Kids' Television Network* during its five-year run, even written some jokes and sketches in the final season when she was only seventeen. She and her castmates had been beloved in the '80s. Like a lot of other flavors from that Rubik's Cube-colored decade, *KTN* was in demand by the adults who'd lived their Izod-clad adolescence through it. She'd been sent a copy of the just-released *Kids' Television Network Volume I* DVD; the Season One cast was featured on the box, and she alone—at fourteen, maybe fifteen—smiled back from an honored place on disc one. She would have a lot of smiling to do this weekend, something she hadn't done since Charlie.

She asked the bellman for ice and drank the gin from the minibar. The bed welcomed her and she nodded off. Her phone's buzzing disturbed her sometime later. A voicemail from Mac. The only adult actor on *KTN*, he'd been a mentor to the young cast. A working actor on stage and screen, he'd put the same effort into the oafish principal in the school sketches as he had in King Lear. But King Lear never made him a star.

"My darling Tristan! I do hope you'll allow me the honor of escorting you to dinner this evening. I believe the reservations are for eight, so I'll meet you in the lobby at seven-thirty. I'll be the handsome gentleman in the brilliant blue scarf. Ta ta!"

Mac's voice left a genuine smile on Tristan's face; it surprised Tristan in the television's reflection. There! Hold on to that!

But how could she hold that smile when her awful story was escaping the dark folds of her mind where she kept it hidden? Thought-stopping was failing. She was trapped with it until the suffocating elevator opened its doors and let her douse it at the lobby bar.

By the time *Kids' Television Network* was canceled in 1986, Tristan was drinking every day. It was easy. While the rest of *KTN*'s cast parlayed their fame into more acting gigs, Tristan wanted out from in front of the cameras, so she tried writing for a while. Pitch meetings were always good for a few drinks. Failing as a writer, she spent a few middling semesters at UCLA, where, at a party, she met the man she would marry a few years later. They were both high on cocaine. He helped her start the talent agency she still runs, but when she was expecting Charlie, left her for a younger woman.

There were bright spots in Tristan's story, Charlie and the sobriety she'd achieved while carrying him first among them. They'd shared a lot of good years; Charlie was a wonderful boy, Tristan stayed sober in—of all places—Hollywood, and her agency flourished. But these bright spots were smoldering of late.

The elevator doors released her. The lobby's modern splendor was stained by geeks: clusters of young people in busy hoodies and sneakers talking too loudly and relaxing too familiarly. But across the room sat Mac, palms on the arms of his chair, wryly smiling, a king amused by a court of jesters. He wore a gray blazer and—as promised—a brilliant blue scarf that complimented Tristan's violet dress. She smiled effortlessly back.

Before she could reach him, a man about her age in a black t-shirt and cargo shorts barred her way.

"Tristan Glass?"

"Yes?"

"Wow! It's really you. I'm a huge fan. Would it be okay if I got a picture?"

The man sidled up to Tristan and extended his arm for a selfie.

When Tristan reached Mac, he said, "Oh, Sweetheart—that was *my* smile you wasted on that awful man!" He tossed his hands into his lap and collapsed his shoulders like a child.

"I'm not sure I did smile," she said. "But I *always* have a smile for you."

Mac rose from his chair and Tristan threw her arms around him. He'd been shaped like an egg standing on its small end: broad-chested, but dainty in the legs. Over time, his egg shape had been inverted: doughy in the seat, withering across the shoulders. They sat and Mac handed her a goblet.

"Club soda with cherries, if I remember correctly," he said. "Thank you."

Mac held up a twin goblet to toast.

"It's so good to see you, Darling," he said. "Things have been rather dreadful lately. Off-Off-Broadway, you know."

"I'm just going to freshen this," Tristan said, holding up her glass.

"My dear, we've barely sat down."

"I'll be just a moment."

When Tristan returned from the bar, Mac picked right back up. "I may be sixty-four, but I can still act circles around men thirty years younger. Forty!"

Tristan sipped gin, relaxed into her chair.

"But how are *you*, Darling?"

Mac had moved to New York after *KTN*, and Tristan lost touch with him for several years. Then, one night after she had put her infant son to bed, the phone rang and there was a warmly familiar, yet melancholy voice. Mac, she quickly realized, was Step-Nining her. She knew the steps from her own recovery, and though she knew it was the wrong thing to do, she interrupted him to tell her own story. Each felt a pleasant rush upon making this connection. Mac's voice shed its blueness and he told her, in his you-would-not-believe-what-happened voice, about how he'd lost the love of his life to AIDS and fallen into depression and addiction and, after hitting bottom and breaking through it with his morose ass, gotten sober. "You must come to New York and celebrate my one-year of sobriety," he'd demanded. "I'm buying you a ticket right now." There'd been more visits, and in-between, regular phone calls (Mac steadfastly refused to use e-mail or Facebook). But they hadn't talked in nearly a year. Not since—

"Charlie died."

"What?"

"He was getting into…" Tristan inhaled sharply. "God, I still don't know what all he'd gotten into. Drinking. Pills. Probably more."

Mac's eyes wetted over. "Oh, that precious boy."

"I thought since I'd stayed sober his whole life, he'd be okay, you know?"

"Sweetheart, you cannot—"

Tristan leaned forward in her chair and placed a palm on Mac's knee. Her own wet eyes looked into his.

"I did a lot more at that age. And for even longer. I couldn't do school, I could barely work, but I never—" Tristan took a drink. "I never looked at death. I think I would've died had

I not quit all that, but even during the worst of it, I never looked at death." Tristan took another drink.

"I'm so sorry. Here I am going on about my career when you've been dealing with this. You poor baby."

"I'm sorry. I've been through all this before with my therapist. And I should've called you."

"Never mind that. Look, if you're not up for dinner, we don't have to go."

"No—I'd like to."

They got into a cab and rode quietly up Lakeshore Drive. Tristan stared across Mac's soft body into the dark plane of the lake; Mac looked there, too.

"I've been drinking gin since I got off the plane," Tristan admitted.

Mac confused his mouth and aired out his nostrils as if confronting a difficult knot.

"No one else knows about Charlie. Please keep my secret."

"I will. But you must stick with me this weekend, okay?"

The director and cast of *Kids' Television Network* played catch-up and swapped plates of appetizers in a private room that barely contained them. Tristan and Mac's entrance brought the room to their feet and set off a roar of applause as if they were guests of honor. Tristan blushed. Mac, always the performer, hiked up his belt, Principal-style, and delivered his catchphrase: "All right you *punks*. You just earned detention!" This gruff utterance was always met with a flurry of spitballs from off-camera. Tonight, Mike, the skinny wiseass, used his straw to send a wet wad of napkin into Mac's cheek.

"That's it, Mr. Tippett," Mac said, his voice returning to its natural timbre, "I'm going to have to expel you!"

Mike stood and shook Mac's hand.

"You're looking good, Old Man," he said.

"And you haven't aged a day."

But Mike had indeed aged a few days; more it seemed than the rest of the cast. He'd grown into a man of obscuring contradictions: He was bulbous and craggy, flushed and faded; to Tristan, he seemed not a day older, and a man with one foot in his grave.

As it were, there weren't two empty seats side-by-side left. Tristan sat next to Mike; Mac was diagonal to her.

"Oh my God, Tristan, you look amazing," Mike said.

"Thank you." Tristan blushed, though she didn't want to. She had seated herself right next to a huge trigger.

Mike had joined the cast in Season Two, a year older than Tristan and many years more worldly. He was detached from the whole *KTN* thing and never really made friends with anyone except Tristan. But when it came time to rehearse and shoot, he was a professional. He sought Mac's instruction, was always asking him questions. And Mac praised him to Tristan. "Watch out," he'd said, "or that young man will take your place as the star." He was half-kidding, but it drove Tristan to her own detachment: This show wasn't *everything*. And what better place to make real her new self than with Mike?

She was in equal parts repulsed and turned on by his black eyes, his anti-prep look, the imprint of tobacco and alcohol on his lips. She bought a new wardrobe from the thrift stores he took her to. She wore thick eyeliner and shadow when he took her to punk shows. Her new world was unabashed in all its qualities: the fashions, the sounds, the violence— all of it was in black overdrive. It was not something you dabbled in. She now understood Mike's determination on set: He lived on eleven. She wanted that, too. She would put anything in her body Mike gave her. Beer, whiskey, pot, pills, coke. They kept this life from the squares at *KTN*. When Mike left after Season Three, Tristan retreated from their scene and back into the Technicolor world of her preppy castmates, but she ached for life on eleven, and found it in what remained: getting high.

Mike raised a cloudy glass—probably whiskey—to his gnarled lips. His black eyes shined too much. Tristan put his life at idling on about five these days.

"So how are you?" Mike asked. "I feel like I've missed so much."

"Let's see…. I was married, but that was a very long time ago. A lovely son."

"Oh, yeah?"

"Charlie."

When Tristan didn't go on, Mike said, "I have a couple daughters. I don't think they care much for me."

What Tristan would give to be living on five! Where was she? On one? When a waitress came around, Tristan asked for whatever Mike was drinking.

"Are you acting? Writing?" Mike asked.

"Talent agency. What about you?"

"Casting."

"You were always good at reading people."

"Could read you, anyway."

Tristan smiled. Her drink came, and she brought it to her lips. From the corner of her eye, she caught Mac catching her. He kept the smile he was wearing for his conversation partner, but his eyes drooped in poor-baby anxiety.

"I'm kind of surprised to see you here," Tristan said. "You were kind of above it all."

"Are you kidding? This was the best time of my life."

"Really?"

"Yeah. We were stars. I never had a better job than being 'Mike' on that silly show. And we had a lot of good times. We'd go out looking so fucked up no one recognized us."

Tristan ordered another drink. She and Mike talked awhile to the others. As the night settled, they returned to each other.

"You can't still listen to that dreadful music?" Tristan asked.

"I'm a pretty simple guy. The same things still get me off." He finished his glass and might've winked at her. "It is what it is."

"Are you going to be okay tonight, Darling?"

Tristan was leaning sleepily against Mac in the cab.

"Yes. I'm going to sleep as soon as I hit the bed."

"Promise you'll stick with me tomorrow. We'll have brunch, sign some autographs, then how about dinner, just the two of us?"

"That sounds nice."

"Promise!"

"I promise."

Versions of Charlie filled the convention floor: prepubescent, hair shagging over ears and neck, drawing mom or dad along; teenage, deflated, slouching through corridors in loud packs.

Tristan hadn't anticipated these ghost-Charlies. She had, upon waking with a brain-sickening hangover, drunk the gin from her minibar and promised that was it. At brunch, she and Mac had made plans for dinner and talked about everything except her relapse, though Mac had assured her that she could call or text him any time she needed. She promised she would. But she hadn't known that not five minutes after arriving at the *KTN* table, the first ghost would announce himself with an echo of her son's laugh, a warm sound that rose, crested, and settled like the opening of a bottle of something carbonated. She wanted to reach out and grab the boy by the bicep, tell him she would do whatever it took to help him get clean.

The ghosts were uninterested in her. While older geeks and some parents who remembered the show shared their memories, the Charlies processed by, their swag bags divining rods to the next must-see booth.

"How're you doing, Kid?"

Mac had arrived to take a spot at the table.

"I'm fine."

Mac turned it on when the first convention-goer, a mother who wanted to hear him do the Principal, recognized him. He was, Tristan realized, showing the way for the other half-dozen cast members present. You're on, he seemed to be saying. Tristan found that it worked: Giving their geeks friendly thanks, writing personal notes rather than just slashing out autographs, posing for multiple pictures—it all helped blot out the ghosts.

"I'm glad you're here," Tristan told Mac during a lull.

Then one of the ghosts approached the table.

"What's this? Who are you?"

Tristan's face stiffened. The kid read the banner, but it failed to return any results.

"Is this an old show? I've never heard of it."

"Beat it, you little shit." Mike had arrived.

"Thank you," Tristan said. "I need something to drink."

"Hair of the dog?" Mike laughed.

Tristan playfully slapped his arm. She wandered the basement room, dodging geeks of every stripe, until she found a concession stand. She bought a large Diet Coke, then found her way to the elevators. When a door opened, she jumped inside and pushed the close-doors button before any ghosts could board. From the minibar in her room, she grabbed rum and poured it into her soda. She stirred the drink with her straw, then fixed the plastic lid back. There.

The ghosts were still on the convention floor. There were cast members she'd not had the chance to speak to last night whom she'd have to deceive today. At opposite ends of the table, telling stories while signing 5x5 postcards of the Season Two cast, were Mac and Mike. She took a seat in the middle of the table, set her cup between her feet, and drew a short line of postcard holders seeking her autograph and a handshake. She could handle it; the sweaty cup between her ankles was a talisman against everything acting upon her, an obfuscating elixir.

Tristan's commitment at the table ended, but she lingered there with some other cast members, Mac and Mike bookending them. The afternoon produced a stream of smiling forty-somethings, sincerely pleased to share a moment with the men and women who had broadcast their teenage anxieties weekly in a burst of jokes and sketches. It reminded her of the times she was recognized by nervously gushing teenagers during *KTN*'s run—which happened a lot, unless she was disguised with Mike. The gratitude worked on her like the rum she'd been sipping, obscuring the pain she'd left home with and the facts of having to return and manage life without Charlie. But eventually, she drew on her straw and got only the rattle of air bubbles, and the flow of fans slowed, their susurrations reduced to occasional clunky outbursts.

Tristan looked to one side and saw that Mac was busy with a fan. His enthusiasm hadn't waned, but he looked worn out. She looked to her other side and as soon as she caught Mike's eye, he got up and approached her. He put his hands on her shoulders and leaned over to whisper.

"Let's go get a drink."

"I shouldn't. I really should take care of some things. My clients don't like me to take time off."

"Don't they know you're the star today? One drink."

At the hotel bar, Tristan drank a G and T; Mike ordered the same. For stretches, they didn't talk, only drank and allowed themselves to settle in their chairs. Something was sloughing off them. They quipped a little about the geeks. Drank another round. Gossiped about the other cast members. Mike asked the waiter for a plate of fries and two beers.

"Mike, please."

"Come on, your figure hasn't changed in thirty years. I think you can share some fries with me. We used to do this all the time."

"You're a bad influence," Tristan said, but smiled.

When the fries and their beers came, the transformation was nearly complete: They could be in a club, fresh riots of noise and smoke, people pogoing.

When they were finished, Mike walked Tristan back to her room.

"I'm going to take a nap. I have a date with Mac in a couple of hours. But that was nice."

Mike kissed her on the temple. "Yeah."

Tristan wasn't in her room for five minutes before she found herself knocking on Mike's door. On the other side were the rhythms of a phone call winding down. Mike opened the door and met Tristan with a surprised flush.

"Tristan?"

Tristan closed the narrow distance between them and kissed his salty lips. The old yin-and-yang of repulsion and attraction bloomed all over her. But, as it had nearly thirty years ago, a need to find—or was it lose?—something within herself tipped the balance.

Tristan woke up cocooned in the bed's thick comforter, the white noise of the AC, and the evening light glowing behind the translucent shades. She was alone. Her mouth was parched.

"Mike?"

Mike called out from the bathroom, where he was brushing his teeth.

"What time is it?"

"Quarter till eight. Mac came by looking for you a while ago."

"Oh, no. He can't see me here."

"I told him we'd had a drink and then you went back to your room to take a nap. Lie of omission, I guess."

There was a voicemail on Tristan's phone. She didn't listen to it.

Mike finally came out of the bathroom. He was in an undershirt and jeans.

"Sleep well?" he asked.

"Yes. I don't know. May I take a shower?"

When Tristan came out of the shower, Mike was sitting on the bed, absentmindedly looking at the *USA Weekend*. There were two full tumblers on the nightstand, little beacons in the darkening room.

Tristan took one and sat on the bed next to Mike. This was clearly Mike's fault, she thought as she nuzzled his great shoulder.

Mike put his hand on Tristan's knee, made tender circles with his thumb.

"Are you and Mac going to paint the town red all night, or can I see you later?"

"Oh, I can't."

"I'm starting to feel a bit used," Mike laughed.

"No—I mean I can't see Mac in this state. He'll understand."

"Then I was thinking of going out to a club. Blues bar? Or maybe find some noisy shit like the old days?"

"Let me go change. You decide."

It was noisy shit. She'd hoped for blues and a boozy descent into obscurity: the slow blacking out of everything except her body humming like struck piano wires under Mike's fingertips. Instead, in a club where it was too loud to talk, Tristan let Mike ply her with draft beer and a pill she swallowed without question. She didn't know what drew forth Mike's smile: the way his hand lay low on the small of her back, the fuzz of sound splitting their heads, or the drugs he'd taken. She'd hoped for an orgasmic eleven; she'd gotten the black overdrive of eleven instead.

At the last, before she'd resigned herself to reliving her teenage nights among the male histrionics of hardcore and sleeping with Mike again before he returned to his wife or girlfriend or pathetic bachelorhood, a question returned to Tristan: Why did Charlie get high? And this question begat further questions: Was there a wound—as he was now her wound—for which getting high was a salve? Or was he seeking something? Was there any difference? It was all deadly reaching. But in the next moment, whatever was oozing through her veins and the pounding and fuzzing noise and Mike's thick hands obliterated her thoughts.

Later, in Mike's room, Tristan felt the dawning of clarity, the ghost of a question she'd been trying to resolve. But exhaustion forced it to go unsettled; Tristan slept.

When Tristan woke up, Mike was showering. Her phone lay pregnantly on the nightstand. There were now two voicemails from Mac. The first expressed, in Mac's excited blushing, that he was waiting for her to meet him for dinner: "But you'll probably be here any second, and I'm getting in a tizzy over nothing!" The second had come much later: "Please call me. I don't care what you're doing or who you're with; I just want to know that you're all right. Love you."

Mike came out of the bathroom wrapped in a towel.

"Good morning," he said softly. "There's coffee for you."

Tristan didn't move. How could she face Mac today? Maybe she could switch to an earlier flight.

"I'd like," Mike began, half dressed, "to see you again. I don't know why we haven't stayed in touch over the years."

Tristan laughed.

"What? My marriage is over, if that's what you're thinking. Long over."

"No. That's not it."

"There a man waiting for you at home?"

"There was only Charlie."

At this, Mike turned away from her and finished dressing.

"I'm sorry," he said.

"For what?"

"For asking you to see me again. I'd really like to see you again, but the timing's all wrong. That's not what this weekend was supposed to be about. You just surprised me when you came into my room yesterday." Mike smiled. "Why didn't you do that back in the day?"

"What do you mean, 'the timing's all wrong'?"
Mike's smile shrunk to a confused ball of lips.
"I know about Charlie. Everyone knows."
"Since when?"
"Since it happened. The whole cast heard. When you didn't cancel, we decided to not bring it up unless you did. We just wanted to give you a nice weekend."
"Mac knew?"
"Of course. He's the one who told me about it. He knew you were never that close with the others, that you'd seek us out. We just wanted to take you back, you know? Make you smile. Is that so bad?"
"I don't know whether to be furious or grateful."
"I've enjoyed the time with you, if that counts for anything."
"I have, too."
"I hope Mac doesn't hate me too much for taking up so much of it. Look, I'm going to get out of here, let you get ready. I'll see you at the panel? Make some people laugh?"
"Okay."
As Mike opened the door, Tristan stopped him.
"Did Mac also tell you I'm an addict?"
Mike paused.
"He didn't mention it. But we can spot our own, can't we?"

Tristan found the hall where the *KTN* panel was about to begin. She found Mike and followed him into the room and up the steps to the dais, where the rest of the *KTN*-ers were seated. She walked over to Mac.
"I'm sorry about last night."
"Don't even think about it. Are you okay?"
"Yeah." Tristan nodded at the crowd. "It's standing room only. The organizers didn't appreciate what great actors they

were dealing with." Tristan kissed Mac on the cheek. "Especially you and Mike."

Over the next hour, the room warmed with laughter as Mac and Mike and all the rest—even Tristan—told the old stories that they hadn't remembered were tucked in their memory banks waiting to be told. The best of them, upon their release into the room, stoked something in Tristan: What she felt couldn't be reduced to a number on a scale or expressions of idleness or overdrive. She felt relief from having to resolve it all, right now. Or ever. What had Mike said? *It is what it is.* She had not had a drink today. She held pictures in her head of being chased around *KTN* sets by Mike, both of them laughing in fits, and hiding behind Mac, who shook his head and smiled at their flirty joy; of baby Charlie nursing, his blue eyes searching her face, his pink mouth separating from her nipple in a gummy smile; of the young man Charlie had grown into, whose flushing smile was treasured more as it became rarer; of her own smile, breaking now for those images and what was still to come.

HIGHWAY STAR

Icky gave a long, low whistle when he saw what was pulling into his garage: A '65 Ford Falcon coupe, bright yellow, sleek fins, whitewall tires, surely a V8 under the hood. Goddamn, it was a fine car. He'd give anything for a ride like that. The driver was some tattooed hipster with greasy black hair who towered over Icky. One of his triceps had a bird that was the same bright yellow as the Falcon, so bright that it had to be new. Icky didn't have any tattoos, but he was curious what a job like that cost. The hipster thought the suspension was out of whack. Would Icky be able to fix it? "Your car's in good hands," Icky said.

When the hipster left, Icky blew off the Astro Van he was working on and got into the Falcon. The leather seat rumbled underneath him when he turned it over. In a second he knew the suspension was a wreck, but he cruised around Jeffersonville for half an hour before taking it back to the garage. It *was* a fine car! He finished the van in a hurry, then put the Falcon on the rack. He worked his hands around the car's underside. He inflated his estimate so he could come down if the driver didn't like the price; he just had to work on this car. He got the driver's voicemail. "Hey, it's Pete Icky. Got an estimate for you. Give me a call."

The hipster didn't call that night. When he hadn't called by ten the next morning, Icky tried him again. "Icky Auto calling again. Would like to give you an estimate and get working on your car." The hipster still didn't call back. For a second, Icky considered taking the Falcon up to the bar that night (he'd been wanting to ask out this one bartender, Sonia) but then he worried the hipster might notice the mileage. He probably had a foot on Icky (who was only five-five) and could've outweighed him by thirty pounds. Best not to take any chances.

The next morning, Icky walked to the café across the street for coffee. While he waited for his coffee, he picked up a *News and Tribune*. It was full of the normal bullshit: Iraq. Afghanistan. Obama. He really couldn't give two shits about any of it. He flipped to the local section. In the obituaries, a familiar face stared back at him. Icky checked the name. It was the hipster! He read the obituary: The hipster was twenty-eight. He had died *at his residence* two nights ago. Icky knew what that meant. What a stupid shit! What could've been so bad that his '65 Ford Falcon couldn't pull him out of his rut? He'd just gotten that new ink, too! Icky couldn't understand suicide. He wasn't living the life he'd thought he would be living at forty (it had always been kind of foggy, but he imagined having more money and maybe a wife), but he'd rather be alive than dead any day of the week. As long as you had a few bucks, there was always something, a drink or a joint or a woman, some little pleasure to numb what ails you. The driver of the Falcon probably had pleasure in spades and didn't know it. Icky turned and looked out the windows toward the shop. There was the Falcon, suddenly orphaned.

Icky didn't call anyone to report that he had the hipster's car. Who would he call, anyway? The police? Every time the phone rang, he thought it would be about the Falcon (he'd left two messages on the hipster's phone) and got ready to play dumb. *Really? That's awful. Yes, I've got the car right here.* But two days passed and no one called. Icky put the Falcon back on the rack and went to work; it was a pleasure to work on that car. When he finished, he took it out for a test drive. It was even better than before. What to do with this beauty? There was no sense in letting it sit around and collect dust, but driving it around town was risky business. Maybe cops were looking for a yellow Falcon with those plate numbers. There was an easy solution: He switched the Falcon's plate with the one on his pickup. Now he felt it was safe to cruise around a bit. The first place he went was his parents' house.

Icky's parents lived a few blocks from Jeffboat, where Pete, Sr. had built ships until his retirement a few years ago. Growing up, Icky and his older sister, Eileen, rode their bikes to where the shipyard ended and a smattering of docks began, and between those docks, they skipped stones and fished and swam (though Icky didn't much like swimming in the river; he didn't like the thought of his toes and—worse—his privates hanging out in the same body of water as the fish and muck that he reeled in on his line). They spent their summers on the banks of the Ohio, making friends and enemies of the other kids who lived nearby, dragging themselves home in the evening stinking of sweat and stale water, their cutoffs sequined with fish scales. But Icky's enchantment with the river didn't survive his adolescence. The excitement of barge launches wore off. The river was valuable to Icky only as a secret place to get high. He fought with his father daily, yelling to his face, in the heat of their worst fight, that he wasn't going to break his back building no stupid ships. Icky floated around his buddies' places, crashing on couches and floors, until he'd worn out all his welcomes, and then spent a couple of restless nights in a sleeping bag down by the river. During the day, he went home to shower and nap. He was big enough to work now and got hired at an oil change place. His father learned of this from his mother and asked him to please come home.

Icky pulled into the drive of his parents' house and blew the Falcon's horn. His mother came to the screen door and eyed the Falcon suspiciously before her son stepped out and patted the car's roof. He brushed his hair from his eyes and gave his naturally wide, open-mouthed smile. He wished he'd changed out of his work clothes.

"Hey, Mom," he said. "Like the new ride?"

His mother approached him like a wave, her arms rising with each step to embrace him at their crest.

"Pete, you don't have to have a special reason to come see us."

"I know, Mom."

"You should come by more often."

When Icky's father appeared at the door, Icky let go of his mother and patted the car's roof again and gave his smile.

"What have you got here?" his father said.

"It's my new ride. Sixty-five Falcon. Excellent condition. Just put new shocks in myself."

His father made his halting gait around the car, peeking in the driver's window at the clean leather interior.

"Almost as nice as my old Gran Torino," he said. Shortly after Icky came back home, his father bought himself a '73 Gran Torino. Icky, as long as he kept his job and didn't bring home any F's, was allowed to take it out on occasion. The third occasion, however, saw Icky get loaded at a girlfriend's and smash the Gran Torino—and the girlfriend—into a tree.

The girlfriend's collarbone was broken, and long after her family had moved out of town, erasing the face of the debt from memory, the Ickys were still paying her medical bills. The poor Gran Torino didn't make it out alive. Icky's wages were garnished until he convinced his father he could stay sober and out of trouble and get his ASE certification. When Icky went to work in his first garage, he started throwing money at the debt again. But since it seemed impossible that he'd ever fully pay it, there was never much accounting on either side, so he eventually stopped. His money seemed better spent trying to forget about the whole ugly mess.

"Let it go," Icky's mother said. "It was over twenty years ago." She turned to Icky. "It's a lovely car. I'll be inside when you two finish out here."

Icky was disappointed that his mother hadn't appreciated the Falcon more. Or appreciated the kind of dough a classic like it cost.

"I didn't know you were doing so well," his father said.

"I'm doing fine. Real fine. People find a mechanic they trust, they stick with him."

"That's the secret of your success? I thought it was inflating your prices."

His father seemed to be kidding him, but Icky was urged to defend himself.

"I treat my customers good, they come back. You want to take the *proof* out for a spin?" Icky held out the keys.

His father waved away the keys. "I don't need to drive it. Fancy cars don't do much for me anymore."

Icky pocketed the keys. "It's some car, though, isn't it?"

"You want to do something for me, come back for dinner tonight. Your sister and her friend are coming, and I'm sure your mother would like to have you, too."

Icky went home and showered and put on a clean t-shirt and pair of jeans. When he returned to his parents', Eileen and her girlfriend's super bikes were parked side by side in the drive. His mother served her special guests in the dining room, where she'd laid out bright linens and, for a centerpiece, a vase containing a single, enormous sunflower. Icky stared into its busy center that seemed to flicker as if it were full of flames. He sat next to his mother, his father sat at the head of the table, and across the table sat Eileen and her girlfriend, Tasha. Icky had understood that Eileen was different from other girls before he knew what "gay" was. When she outgrew the river, she continued to wear jeans and loose-fitting shirts. For her senior pictures (voted Class of '87's Most Outgoing Senior), she wore a men's blazer over a Culture Club t-shirt. She never "came out"—one day she just brought home a girl she'd met at the local IU, and it was clear to everyone that they were a couple. This was almost twenty years ago, and there had been a handful of girlfriends since then.

Icky paid no attention to Eileen and Tasha's gossip about the marketing firm Eileen worked for. There'd been layoffs, but Eileen had seniority; in work, as in everything else, she was a rock that wouldn't be moved. Icky's father didn't seem to be keeping up with the conversation either, and his mother only made little noises of agreement or disdain. Icky dipped forkfuls of his salmon patty into the pool of melted butter in his mashed potatoes, waiting for the moment he could excuse himself and go out in the Falcon. He wanted to go to the bar. If he could park the Falcon on the street in view of the door, he was going to ask out Sonia.

Eileen was speaking to him. "How much did that big banana set you back?"

"What?"

"Your Yellow Submarine. How much did you pay for it?"

"Please," Icky's mother said. "Let's not talk about money at the table."

Icky searched his father's craggy face for any interest in the question, even before he considered how he might answer it.

"Come on," Eileen pleaded. "I'm curious."

"Mom's right," Icky said. "I never asked you what you dropped on that rice burner."

"Oh, just tell us."

Icky waved his free hand at nothing. "It was nothing I couldn't handle. A few grand."

"'A few grand'? Like, fifteen grand? Or three grand?"

Icky smirked. "Three grand? Come on."

"Did you find it around here?" Icky's father asked.

"What do you mean?"

"Was the seller from around here?"

"Yeah." Icky was getting flustered. His mashed potatoes were thick in his mouth; he felt the panic of choking rise and then dissipate. He took a drink of water. "Look, it just kind of fell in my lap. It's some car though, there's no doubt about that."

From his parents' house, Icky cruised up Spring Street, passing the low, red brick building where the bar was, turned around a few blocks before the police station, then turned back up Spring when he hit the river. He made this circuit several times, scanning the radio as he went. As luck would have it, he caught two of his favorite songs about driving: "Highway Star," by Deep Purple, and "Radar Love," by Golden Earring. He bopped his head and drummed his thumbs on the wheel, checking himself when he crept by the bar. He didn't want to show up too early (Sonia might mistake him for one of the lonely men who started drinking as soon as the bar opened) or too late (he wanted to beat the crowd to assure himself of both a seat at the bar and a prime parking spot). Parking real estate was going fast, though, so he eased the Falcon into his dream spot (directly across from the door!), got out, buffed his fingerprints off the door with a handkerchief, and stepped into a dive on his side of the street. He steeled himself with two shots of bourbon. He hated to drop any money here; your tip budget grew exponentially when you bar hopped, and he was going to be generous with Sonia tonight. But he needed something to set him straight before he faced her.

His bar greeted him with the dry stink of the smoke-saturated walls (even years after the ban) and the sweet and savory smells of big pots of marinara and things just pulled from the deep fryers. A few diners lingered over wine or coffee. Sonia was tending bar. Her yellow scoop-neck tee showed off a good amount of skin. A little silver cross rested above her breasts. Even in the bar's scattered light, Sonia's blue eyes were brilliant; if you met them while ordering, your thoughts were knocked off course and you couldn't remember whether you wanted a Blue Moon or a Boilermaker. Icky had been talking her up for weeks. She was guarded, but that was to be expected from a bartender who had every creep in town hitting on her. But from what he gathered she was fiercely independent; she'd never married, had no children or other liabilities, and owned a house somewhere nearby. She must've taken home a fortune every weekend. The only other way a gal like her could make that kind of money was by taking her clothes off—which to Icky was the best-paying job for the least amount of *work*. It's not like they're building ships.

Icky took a seat at the bar. He smiled at Sonia as she worked her way over to him.

"What are you smiling about, Pete?" she asked.

"I want to show you something." He nodded toward the door. "See what's out there?"

A group of men walked in from smoking cigarettes, and when the path to the door was clear you could see the Falcon, shining brightly under a streetlight.

"What am I supposed to be looking at? That big yellow car?"

"Yes, the car," Icky said with maybe a little too much excitement. "That's my new Falcon. Just bought it."

"It's very nice."

"It's some car."

"What can I get you to drink?"

Icky ordered a beer and let Sonia go. She clearly wasn't that impressed by the Falcon. She needed to know that a classic like it, in the shape it was in, didn't come cheap—that not any river-stinking Jeffboat worker or needle-dick cop could afford a ride like it. But he knew better than to offend her by coming right out and saying it. He ordered more beers. Asked her how things were going. Said he was busier than ever at the garage, but that he was glad to have all the business (nodding toward the Falcon). Nothing seemed to get her attention. Resigned to leave without getting a date with her, he paid his tab and left a tip, though it wasn't as generous as he'd planned. He said, "Take care," and left.

The Falcon rumbled to life underneath him. Goddamnit! He was a man of means, a man with a fine car. He was going to ask Sonia out. She could turn him down because he was short and had an ugly face, but she would not deny him because he wasn't a man of means.

He turned off the engine and marched back across the street to the bar. He wedged between two men for Sonia's attention.

"What is it, Pete?"

"How'd you like to go out sometime in the Falcon? Anywhere you want."

"Have you always driven nice cars like this?"

"Sure. I had a '73 Gran Torino before this. This car suits me better."

Icky had picked up Sonia outside her house. They were going across the river to Louisville for dinner. That afternoon, Icky had waited in line at his bank for twenty minutes, furiously scraping the grease from beneath his nails to pass the time. Why in hell did they close all but one teller window at lunch? When the tight-ass chick finally called him to the window, he requested his balance, stared for a moment at the amount lightly inked on the slip, and budgeted for his date with Sonia. He wrote a check for CASH and handed it over to the gatekeeper. As she counted the cash for him, he reached inside the window for a butterscotch, not realizing until the candy was in his jaw that, based on how far inside the window the bowl sat, it wasn't intended for customers. The teller glared at him. To hell with her. The cash was now in Icky's wallet, separated by the bank slip into the minimum he'd need for dinner and drinks and extra in case things went really well.

Before they got on the bridge, Icky had to stop to fill up the Falcon.

"Sorry about this," he said. "You need anything?"

Sonia laughed. "What could I need? We're going to dinner."

Sonia watched Pete jog up to the station to prepay for his gas. He wore a black denim shirt and dark jeans. He was a cute guy, a little goofy, and not the brightest man she'd ever gone out with. But probably not the dumbest, either. There was something at once sad and hopeful about his face; his smile, a brave show of crooked and stained teeth, always looked as if it could break away at any second.

Sonia became aware of three young men in front of the station admiring Pete's car. They were the dressed-in-black types that closed her bar down on the weekends. Their interest in the car was palpable; they pointed and talked over top of each other.

When Pete returned to pump the gas, she said, "Your car has got some fans."

"What's that?" Pete asked, inserting the nozzle.

"Those boys over there. They're practically drooling over your car."

Icky cocked his head toward the station. Oh fuck fuck fuck. Okay, there was a chance those greasy shits were genuinely admiring the Falcon for what it was: a goddamn classic. But Icky's guts fell and told him there was an infinitely greater chance they recognized the Falcon as their dead buddy's missing car.

"I'm going to run in after all," Sonia said, "for some water."

Icky was left alone pumping gas into the Falcon. He kept the men in the corner of his eye, but that didn't keep them at bay. They formed a semicircle around the Falcon, checking out the wheels, the plate. One man laid his hands on the roof and peeked through the passenger window.

"This is a real fine car you've got," he said.

"Thanks," Icky said. "It's some car."

The man in the rear said, "Did you get this car around here?"

"I'd love to know where you came across this beauty," the other one said.

"I've had it a while," Icky said. "Years."

"We had a friend who had one just like this," the first man said. "We thought maybe you took it off him."

Icky glanced at the digital readout on the pump. The change flashed hysterically, but the dollars wouldn't tick off fast enough. $8, $9, $10.

"Are you sure you didn't take it off a guy around here?"

"I got it someplace else. I don't remember much about the fella who sold it to me."

$11, $12.

"You'd remember our friend. Had a lot of tattoos. A big, yellow bird on one arm. You'd never forget it."

Icky's mouth was bone dry. He shrugged. At $15, he returned the nozzle and slid into the Falcon. The men crowded around his window. One grabbed the handle; another pulled him off. "Not here," he said. "Too many people around. Let's follow him."

The men walked toward their car, but the first man protested. "He's gonna get away!"

"He's not going anywhere till his girlfriend comes back."

The attendant's voice called out from the pump that Icky had paid for twenty dollars' worth. Sonia was pushing open the station's glass EXIT door.

Icky started the engine and pulled away, tires squealing.

The men scrambled into their car—a Gran Torino! Icky's first thought was to head to the garage, but he had two vehicles in there already, and the men weren't that far behind, so he'd never have time to park the Falcon, move a car from the garage, and then put the Falcon inside. His mother always parked her car in his parents' garage, and how would he explain what he was sticking his car in their garage for anyway? His only hope was to lose them, ditch the Falcon (remembering to remove his plate), and walk home. No one would ever know he'd had the car. And hell, in a few years, as long as they were good years, maybe he could replace it anyway. It was a source of comfort that he decided to put away some money (starting with reallocating the cash in his wallet) for a new vehicle. The Falcon was just a test drive.

He was weaving through traffic, trying to lose the men and not draw attention to himself. He had no destination, but imagined he had a better chance of escape if he headed north out of the city. In a few minutes, the squat, brick buildings of downtown gave way to flat, industrial sites. The roads opened up. He turned onto a four-lane highway and pushed the Falcon harder than he'd yet had the chance to; he would've enjoyed it if he weren't being chased! The sun was falling fast, and Icky wondered if he could stay ahead of the men until dark. It would be easier to escape that way, but if he was caught, it would be easier for them to give him what he had coming without any witnesses.

He wasn't a gambling man, so when the distance between him and his pursuers was at its widest, he took a sharp left onto a gravel road that led into woods. It pained Icky so much to hear the pings of the Falcon's tires throwing gravel into its underside that he slowed down, even as he saw the men close in behind him. The road was turning out to not be much of a road at all—only a service road winding upward to somewhere. In a moment, the road straightened and a clear path through the trees revealed a great fireball at the end of the line. Icky squinted and pushed on.

At the end of the line, he wasn't consumed by flames; he slammed the brakes and skidded to the edge of what he now knew was the quarry. His heart felt enlarged as it pumped behind his ribcage. He turned off the Falcon, left the key in the ignition. There was no time to get choked up about losing her. He got out, saw the men pull in behind him. Icky looked into the pool below him. He remembered kids talking about sneaking up here, diving and swimming. How far down was it? A hundred feet? More? It seemed like suicide!

The men got out of their car. The crunch of their boots in the gravel sounded like breaking bones. The woods on either side of Icky were thick with summer. He took another look into the water.

He took a few steps toward the men, as if to take his punches, then turned and made a running leap over the edge. The fall was mercifully short; he cut the water feet first and was squeezed by a cold fist. He thrashed around until he'd brought his face to the surface, then started sucking in air. He took on a mouthful of water. Never was much of a swimmer. He hadn't been broken apart on the rocks, as he thought was a real possibility, but now he thought he might drown. Exhaustion drained every inch of him. His flailing arms and legs were giving out. He wasn't sure of the best direction to swim in. And his clothes weighed him down. He started stripping them off: His shirt floated away, his shoes sank, he wriggled from his jeans. He held his wallet in his teeth as he started paddling, but he was taking on mouthfuls of water. *I'm gonna drown. I'm gonna drown!* He unclenched his teeth. Tried to breathe. Paddled. Breathed. Paddled. He was getting somewhere.

OEDIPUS, REX

Junior year, Rex transferred to SoCal, started every game behind the plate, and won Most Outstanding Player in the College World Series. In the championship game, he was the only hitter who could puzzle out what Theo Spinks—easily the best D-1 starter that season—was throwing and crushed his knuckleball into left-center for the game-winning RBI. His teammates lifted him upon their shoulders. He felt like a king.

Rex carried that feeling into senior year. A real BMOC. But people talked and it caught up to him in the spring. Cassie pressed him on it. They were in her room, the roommate out, a bra on the doorknob. Nearly undressed, and she started asking him about this girl and that girl and she clearly wasn't liking what she was hearing, no matter how much Rex assured her it was different with her.

"It's different with you."

"But you were still *with* all of them! That's so disrespectful to me!"

"I didn't even know you existed!"

"You should've thought of that, you disgusting pig!"

Cassie thrust his jeans and shirt into his arms and shoved him out the door.

"My sneakers!" he said, but she wouldn't open back up.

On the way back to his apartment, he stopped at a party on Greek row to drown his humiliation and pain.

"Where are your shoes, Rex?"

Rex ignored the question and the sideways looks and whispers of partygoers, and camped out by a keg till it was nothing but foam. Leaving, he stumbled down the house's front steps, landed on his right foot all wrong, and fractured a metatarsal.

"Isn't your cousin Jo getting a degree in physical therapy? Have her come look at it."

That was Rex's mother on the phone back in Delphi, Indiana. Rex didn't immediately heed her advice; he'd known his cousin was a grad student at the university, but neither of them had ever gotten in touch with the other. They'd never been close. She was older and very square. They had nothing in common except blood.

But Rex's foot swelled to enormous proportions, and his treatment of ibuprofen, Tylenol, and Budweiser wasn't helping, so he called her up. She came by the next afternoon with a duffel of compression bandages and ointments and suggested that they get right to it.

"Let's see what we're dealing with here." Sitting on the sofa opposite him, she took his foot in her hands. They were cold and impersonal. "How'd you do this again? Basketball?"

There'd been no small talk, no niceties. Nothing to suggest Jo was interested in seeing her cousin, nor anything that approached a pleasant bedside manner. Not that Rex was particularly interested in her outside of what she could do to help him get back in the game. But still.

"Baseball. But that's not how it happened. I tripped."

"Tripped?"

"Down some stairs. Leaving a party."

Jo smirked. "Exactly why I never got serious with anyone as an undergrad."

Jo massaged Rex's foot, her hands warming. As her fingers searched the swollen mass, her eyes fixated on something above Rex's head. His Cubs pennant? A smudge on the wall? Rex caught himself looking at her as she searched/stared. She was more attractive than he'd remembered or expected. She had deep brown eyes and striking dark curls pulled into a tight ponytail. But what most stood out were her shoulders, which he could tell through her t-shirt were lean and strong. All that work with her hands.

After a few moments, Jo seemed satisfied to have found whatever she was searching for and began to work more earnestly. Her fixed gaze loosened and she looked at her cousin. "You're going to have to lay off this thing for a while."

Rex looked away; there was something unsettling about her eyes. "How long?"

"Depends. I see you've got crutches. Keep using them."

Something on an end table caught her attention. It was Rex's Intro to Drama textbook, which was open to *Oedipus the King*, which Rex hadn't looked at in days.

"Oedipus," Jo said.

"You read that?"

"Sophomore year, I think."

Rex swept his hand over his head. "Over my head."

"I can give you the Cliffs Notes. Oedipus' parents believe he's going to grow up to kill his father and marry his mother, so they nail his feet together and leave him on a hill to die."

"Ouch." Rex wiggled his swollen foot. "This doesn't seem so bad, now."

"Oedipus means 'swollen foot.' Anyway, an old man saves his life, and he's adopted by another couple. Long story short, the prophecy comes true: He ends up killing his father and marrying his mother."

"Well, that's gross."

Jo said something like, "Is this good for you?" and Rex narrowed his eyes in confusion.

"Is this time good for you?"

"For what?"

"You're going to need weeks of PT. I'm free at this time. Are you?"

"I'm not going anywhere."

"I'll see you next week, then." Jo nodded toward Rex's crutches. "Stay on three feet."

After that first session, Jo was never far from Rex's thoughts. His aching foot was a constant reminder of her, but there was something else. As the time approached for Jo to return the following week, Rex admitted what he'd been denying since she'd walked into his apartment: He was attracted to her. Against both reason—she was his cousin, for shit's sake—and all physical indicators that urged him away from the thought—clammy hands, something like nausea in his solar plexus—there it was.

There was a knock on the door, and Rex hobbled over on his crutches to answer. Jo was there, duffel hanging on her shoulder, and this time she smiled. It was an opening of sorts—at least that's how he read it—to entertain his desire, which he was now sure of: as sure as the weight of a fastball in the pocket of his mitt, as his grip on the bat when his arms reached full extension, as the feel of dirt under his cleats when he rounded second.

Jo sat down and waited for Rex to extend his foot to her. "What's the matter?" she said.

"Nothing." Rex gave her his foot, and to distract himself—he was certain he shouldn't enjoy it—he asked her about Oedipus again. "Does Oedipus know he's marrying his mother?"

"Of course not."

"What's he do when he realizes it?"

"She kills herself. He… let's see… oh, he gouges out his eyes. Are you all right, cousin?"

Rex must've been shuffling in his chair, wriggling his foot. How could he just sit there with his desire for her? It was a curse!

"How's he end up killing his father?"

Rex finally got back on two feet, and even though there was still too much pain to squat behind the plate, Coach put him in to pinch hit a few times. And thanks to some of his clutch singles, it looked like they were heading to another world series. All this in spite of his physical therapy being cut short by several weeks.

In what would be Rex's final game, Coach put him in with two outs in the ninth. They were two runs down with a man on second. The clichéd dream of every kid who ever tossed a ball in the air to bat it over the backyard fence. Rex had acted it out a thousand times; sometimes he knocked it over the fence and sometimes he struck out. So much pathos on those evenings back in Delphi! Now he stepped to the plate, eager for a real-life win, and whiffed the first two pitches. Pivoting on his back foot was killer. He calmed down. The whole thing with Jo was over, anyway. He shouldn't be off his game for that. He'd greeted her at the door and tried—oh, how could he have stooped to such a shameful thing!—to kiss her. She'd pushed him away, and he'd lost his balance and fallen to his hands and knees. "You're disgusting!" she'd said.

Out of a well of restraint that he hadn't drawn from as he clumsily pawed at his cousin, Rex drew four balls and shuffled down to first, the tying run. The next batter hit the ball to deep right. Rex rounded second, the pain in his foot shooting all the way to his eyeballs. He rounded third.

"He was an angry guy," Jo had said of Oedipus. "When this old man blocks his path, he murders him. That was his father."

The catcher was a wall before the plate. He already had the throw. Rex was all shoulder and knee as he barreled into him. The impact was a violent shutting and opening of bodies: Rex's folded in on itself, and the catcher was cracked open and laid on his back. Though he looked dead to the world—even a semblance of a chalk outline from the remains of the batter's box—the catcher lifted his mitt, and Blue threw up his fist. But Rex couldn't see this. The collision had knocked him blind. He writhed in the dirt, fetally. Then he heard the merciful sounds of a chorus of his teammates: "You looked like you were trying to kill him!" "Can you see, Rex?" "C'mon, Rex, let's get you out of here." He could do nothing but let them save him from himself.

PRAY FOR HER

The bulletin board, lovingly constructed by one of Jack MacKaye's freshmen, Sam Schumer, showed a world map, each continent faithfully cut from colored paper and glued to a sheet of blue, onto which was traced the journey of Aimee Airington, the sixteen-year-old sailor attempting to circumnavigate the world. A photo, which Sam had taken from her blog, of Aimee sitting on her sailboat, her blue eyes looking dreamily past you, her signature red jacket and blond hair blowing in the breeze, was set in the center. At different points along the line of her journey, Sam had posted brief, typed updates. Jack touched his finger to the last update in the middle of the Indian Ocean: This was where, two days ago, Aimee disappeared. The story was everywhere. Boys who had tormented Sam for his crush now showed reverence when passing the bulletin board. It was only in the morning before the students arrived that Jack dared touch Sam's shrine.

Sam and the rest of the boys, the other teachers, maybe everyone in the world, were praying for Aimee's safety. But Jack was hoping she'd never come up from the place in the ocean where he was holding her down with his fingertip.

He would scarcely have known about Aimee Airington were it not for Sam. Her attempt at circumnavigation was a story he'd seen online and not clicked on; that must've been in January. Soon after, Sam wanted to make an announcement during class, and Jack obliged. Because it was Jack's first year and because he'd gone to public schools, being among the Trinity boys was like being in a foreign country and, while he clung firmly to his history lessons, he deferred to them in all matters of protocol. He thought Sam was going to tell his classmates about the bulletin board he'd put together and be back in his seat in about ten seconds, but the kid gave a five-minute speech. He explained the bulletin board—every day he would mark the young sailor's progress—and then paraphrased her bio from her website. The boys got fidgety as the talk stretched out. Jack pitied the kid; even among a roomful of mostly freshmen, Sam was small. His face was unblemished and perfectly hairless, like a young girl's. His blazer ate him. And he was badly in need of a haircut. At the end of his speech, he tossed his last hope for social acceptance overboard by pumping his fist and shouting "Go Aimee!"

The bulletin board drew a lot of attention from the other teachers and staff. Several athletes got into it, too. All through the spring, they followed Aimee's journey through Sam's updates: from her launch in California, down the Pacific and around Cape Horn, across the Atlantic toward Cape Town. Jack felt obligated to agree whenever another teacher said, "What an inspiring kid," or "Amazing, huh?" But he barely heard what they were saying. His niece's arrival last fall had dampened his ability to focus.

One afternoon after Aimee had been at sea for a couple of months, Jack found Sam after school posting an update. The kid stayed after school for a half dozen academic clubs, but excused himself whenever his project called.

"She's about to finish crossing the Atlantic."

"That's great, Sam. When should she wrap this thing up?"

"August."

Jack dug his hands into his pockets and moved closer to the bulletin board. Sam finished applying the update and stepped back so that he and his teacher seemed to admire his work together.

"Do you sail?" Jack asked.

"No."

"Do your parents have some kind of boat on the Ohio?"

"No. They golf."

"So you don't have any sea legs. Why are you so interested in this sailor?"

Sam turned a stung look his way. Then he looked at Aimee's picture. "Well, it's amazing what she's doing, you know. Sailing around the world by herself."

"Sure."

"And… she's following her dream."

"What's your dream, Sam? Something like this?" Jack pointed at the bulletin board. "Climbing some mountain or something?"

"I don't know. I might like to be an ambassador. Or in the U.N."

"Well, do well here, get into a good college. You know that already."

"Was your dream to be a teacher?"

Jack gazed at the red paper cutout of North America, his eyes going blurry at the Midwest. He took off his glasses and pressed his thumb and forefinger into his sockets. "I don't remember."

"I'd better get going." Sam started to walk away.

"I remember now," Jack called out. "I wanted to be the starting shortstop for the Reds."

Sam turned around. "Were you close?"

"Not even."

Jack's home since finishing his master's was a two-bedroom apartment in a brick building with quiet tenants. For one week last August, he'd enjoyed waking up early, listening to NPR while he ate breakfast, and walking the two miles to Trinity; a zigzag of streets led him by well-tended homes and houses turned into offices and salons. His route was thick with trees and their blessed shade. Then his sixteen-year-old niece, Leigh-Anne, moved in. Now he had to make sure she was up in the morning and ready for school; she wasn't easily roused, but once she was up and showered and dressed, she talked over *Morning Edition* about nothing he could follow—a crazy person she and her friends saw, something someone tweeted. She wore jeans and hippie-looking tops or t-shirts of bands he didn't know, and all her clothes, he noticed when he went to the basement to do laundry, emitted a ripe, earthy smell when touched. Her face, which as a little girl had been like polished ivory, was uninterrupted from ear to ear with dark freckles and silver objects: studs sprouting above her lips and eyes and in her nose, hoops dangling from her ears. Bunches of black curls hung about her busy face. She ate nothing for breakfast but a handful of dry cereal and pills from a prescription bottle and washed that down with a swig from a two-liter of Coke. Then he drove her to school. She changed NPR to New Rock. There wasn't time to drive home and enjoy his walk to Trinity, so Jack drove and arrived early.

Jack grew used to his students. They were not unlike himself and the boys he'd known in school: Even in their uniforms he could identify the socially mobile boys, the rebellious boys, the awkward boys (like Sam), and the boys who floated politely through the halls and classrooms (like

Jack had). The boys' personalities often ballooned against their uniforms: Polo or another logo on the left breast of the particularly well-to-do boys' pressed shirts, loose knots in the ties of the faux-hawked "punks." But they all wore the sheen of privilege like a stain they were unaware of. While Jack knew it wasn't their fault, he couldn't help harboring a distaste for the boys as a whole, even though he liked certain individuals. He could even say, with few exceptions, that he liked all the students in his classes; they were always attentive to his history lessons, usually earnest in their work, and sometimes even genuinely interested in the subject at hand.

It made him wonder what in the hell was going on over at Leigh-Anne's school. Though it probably was just Leigh-Anne. The afternoon after Jack had run into Sam in the hall, he stayed at school late and then went to the grocery (he'd texted Leigh-Anne—she didn't listen to voicemails—to tell her he'd bring home a pizza for dinner). When he arrived, his niece was sitting at the kitchen table, her legs pulled in close and her bare feet hanging over the edge of her chair. She was smoking a joint. His bourbon was on the table next to a tumbler of melting ice.

"What's going on?" Jack said. "Having a cocktail while you wait for dinner?" He pointed at the joint she was holding over her knees. "And where'd you get this?"

"Somewhere. Put that pizza down, I'm starving."

Jack set down the pizza and draped his blazer over the back of his chair. He held a hand out for the joint and took a hit before handing it back. He made himself a strong drink.

"Lucas has been hooking up with my now ex-friend, Jules. That's why I'm getting fucked up."

"Let me ask you something."

"Is it *why is Lucas a giant asshole?* Or *why is Jules such a slut?* I don't know."

"What do you think of Aimee Airington?"

"Who?"

"The girl sailing around the world. You know who I'm talking about, right?"

"Spell it for me." Leigh-Anne picked up her phone and thumbed the name on the QWERTY keys. "Oh yeah, I saw this on Twitter."

"Well, what do you think about it?"

"I don't know." Leigh-Anne squinted at the screen, skimming the story. "How does she have enough to eat for that long?"

"I'm not sure. I'm curious how her doing that makes you feel, since you're the same age and all."

"Seems impossible that she could take enough to eat."

Jack released an exasperated breath. "You're getting caught up on details I don't know anything about. I just want to know what you think about it. About her attempting to sail around the world at sixteen."

Leigh-Anne set down her phone and picked up a slice of pizza. "I wouldn't want to do it. Be alone all that time. Sounds boring."

"So, you're not impressed?"

"I don't know. I guess so. I just don't see why you'd want to do that." She finished off the joint. "Like, what's the point?"

Jack picked up his bourbon. "Go easy on this stuff, all right? It's a school night, for Christ's sake."

And then Aimee disappeared in the Indian Ocean. This time, when the story appeared, Jack clicked on it. He expected Sam would be a wreck, but the kid arrived in his classroom early, as usual, took his seat, and opened his notebook to a fresh page. Jack asked him what he thought had happened. Sam said Aimee had been caught in a storm, which was to be expected, and that satellite contact had been lost, but he was confident she was perfectly safe; the worst, he seemed sure of, was that she'd been blown slightly off course. Her journey might take a few more days. He was going to wait to hear from her before updating his bulletin board.

It was the next day, after Jack had secretly wished for Aimee to never come back, that the school's optimism began to wear away. The teachers and students who'd taken the greatest interest in Aimee talked solemnly in the halls. Some boys wanted to do something.

The next day, Friday, a prayer vigil for Aimee—organized by Sam—was announced for Saturday night. Sam asked Jack to come.

Jack didn't expect to find Leigh-Anne at home; most Fridays she stayed out until after he'd gone to sleep and then spent half of Saturday in bed. But he heard noises from her room. She'd never brought a girlfriend over, and Jack debated knocking, finally deciding he ought to at least see who was in there with her. Maybe it was Jules, and the girls were making up. But when he was let inside, Leigh-Anne was alone. She was lying back on a pile of pillows on her bed, thumbing at her phone. Her stereo—an old one Jack had given her—was playing something screamy to her scattered clothes and magazines and a Leinenkugel she had plundered from the fridge.

"Are you going out tonight?" Jack asked.

"I don't know."

Jack looked at the sea of balled-up t-shirts and issues of *SPIN* and *Alternative Press*; not even a footpath to

Leigh-Anne's bed had been carved out of the clutter. It made him motion sick. How many hundreds of dollars of this stuff (and where did she get her money?) and the girl didn't really have a thing.

"How'd you like to go to the mall and let me get you some new clothes?"

"What?" Leigh-Anne laughed, out of flattery or embarrassment, Jack didn't know.

"I just thought you might like to go shopping, that's all. Do you need anything?" Jack felt that embedded in the graffiti print of her nylon track jacket was an insult directed at him. "Besides, I don't think I've bought you anything since you were little."

"I guess I could use some things. How about just giving me the money and letting me go shopping. That's what Grandma and Grandpa do."

And you spend it on trash, Jack wanted to say. For Christ's sake, don't start spending it on shit to snort up your nose, shit to pump in your veins.

"All right. But buy something nice with it. Go to the Gap."

Leigh-Anne laughed again. She took a drink of her beer.

"You can borrow the car tomorrow if you'll do that. But no drinking and driving. I've got to go to a prayer vigil for Aimee Airington."

"Who?"

"The sailor. The girl. Ring any bells? She's lost at sea."

"She's lost? Do you think she's dead?"

"Christ, I don't know. I honestly don't care."

"Really?"

"Like you said: What's the point?"

The prayer vigil was held on the football field. From his darkened classroom where he was hiding out, Jack watched as boys and their families lined up at the gate to receive a candle and a small, printed prayer; like the bulletin board, these prayers were carefully prepared by Sam. Jack imagined the sea of tiny, hopeful lights spreading across the yard lines and the glowing, solemn faces turning toward the home stands where Father Maguire, Trinity's spiritual advisor, was about to speak. Jack didn't pray—didn't believe in it. And he could not believe in it now, after he'd failed to pray when his family needed it most, when his sister was killing herself.

There were small footsteps in the hall.

"Mr. MacKaye?" Sam held two unlit candles in his hands.

"Sam."

"Why are you sitting in the dark? It's about to start."

"You go on, Sam. I'll be along."

"I'll wait for you."

Jack asked Sam to sit down.

"Don't you think it's unfair," Jack said, "that Aimee Airington, just because she's born to the right people, gets to sail around the world when she should be in school?"

"She's homeschooled, actually."

"That's not the point, Sam. I'm asking if you ever think about why she gets her own sailboat before she's old enough to drive and gets the whole world's attention when she tries to sail around the world."

Sam frowned. He clearly didn't understand.

"She gets all that—and what do normal kids get?"

"Are you saying I should be jealous of her?"

"I don't know. You're a Trinity boy, you're special enough." Jack raised his hand high to form a line in the air. "Aimee Airington is up here, okay. One of the luckiest kids to ever live. Has got the money and the support to—what did you say? Follow her dream. And you're here," he lowered his hand to eye level. "You've got it good. Parents send you to a good school, have a college fund set aside for you. I doubt they'd let you leave school to try some crazy feat, but still. Other kids… other kids don't even know if their parents love them. So they sleep around and take every drug they can get their hands on, just looking for something to make them feel right. And nothing works. Nothing works, Sam. They're down here." He slammed his palm on his desk. Sam winced. "They're sooner dead than feeling right." Jack turned toward the window. The football field was aglow. "The whole world loves your precious Aimee. She doesn't need me."

The vigil's glow had drawn Sam outside. Jack didn't follow him. His car was still parked at his apartment building; Leigh-Anne had either not gone shopping or she was already back. Jack imagined the $150 he'd given her blown on t-shirts from Hot Topic. Or weed. Why'd he let her have it? It would be all right if she'd bought just one nice thing. A summer dress from the Gap, or wherever kids shopped these days, could be the thing that began to turn her away from making the same mistakes as her mother. He wanted her to wake up to the world, to go to college, to find joy. At the least, he wanted her to not leave him and her grandparents wondering every day if they were going to get a call telling them she was dead. If only he found her modeling her new dress, she would be okay.

The television lit up the empty living room. Jack called out for Leigh-Anne. From her room sprinted a shirtless boy whose eyes were hidden under pitch-black bangs; a flash of ribs and denim slid past Jack and out the door before he was aware of what was happening. Leigh-Anne appeared outside her door with a scream, pulling her t-shirt down to cover her naked bottom. Her white legs glowed in the dark hallway, startling Jack; her adult legs, which he'd never seen, were the ivory she'd been as a child. Nothing was said for a minute. Then Leigh-Anne turned to go into her room.

"Wait," Jack said. "We have to talk about this."

Leigh-Anne spoke quietly, perhaps even with remorse: "I'm just getting my underwear."

Jack followed her to the door, and then waited as she went inside to find her underwear among the hoard on her floor. He began to speak, embarrassed to be heard saying what he needed to say—to be playing father. "I said your girlfriends could come over but I never said anything about boys. You should've asked me first. What were you thinking?" From inside her room, Leigh-Anne groaned. "You're sixteen. You shouldn't be doing this stuff already."

Leigh-Anne finally came back to the hallway to face Jack.

"I'm sorry," she said. "I should've asked if Lucas could come over tonight. But it's not like I don't know what I'm doing."

"You *don't* know what you're doing. But it's not your fault. No one's ever shown you."

They were both struck dumb by Jack's words. How would they move forward? Would they be stuck in the dim hallway forever?

The television volume was suddenly raised by the urgent pitch of a news anchor: Aimee Airington had made contact. She was unharmed. She was coming home.

"That's good," Leigh-Anne said. "Isn't that good?"

"Yeah, that's good. Let's go watch."

DREAM OF THE AMBULOCETUS

The Ambulocetus slinks toward the river's edge, spine flexing upward into a conifer's lowest boughs, knees weary with walking, snout scenting spent needles and brackish water. He does not hesitate as he breaks the plane of the water's surface and disappears from terra firma. In the shallow water, his back undulates in great arcs, his forward motion fueled by thrusts of his webbed feet. His small forelimbs steer him. He's hungry.

He swims the width of the river and settles in the muck of the opposite bank so that his great snout is just submerged and aimed landward. He waits for prey. And waits.

A small mammal ambles into his field of vision. It pokes at the muddy shore for prey, crunches an insect in its jaws. The Ambulocetus knows that the creature remains vigilant even as it chews its food, watching and listening for that which would flip it from predator to prey. But the Ambulocetus is deathly still until the moment he strikes, launched by his webbed feet from the soft bottom. His jaws collapse where his senses told him the prey was—but the creature is dashing from the bank on its hooves, skittering through conifers for safety.

The Ambulocetus sinks back into the river; there is no point in giving chase in the forest. His squat, splayed limbs are no good at moving his long, quarter-ton body with any grace or speed on land. On land, he is a terrible hunter.

Worse, he is terribly vulnerable to predators—enormous, clawed mammals who stalk the forests for flesh.

He retreats from the murky shallows into the deeper, clearer water in the middle of the river. Here, he is the top predator, his long jaws opening to ensnare fish. Here, in the cool give of the water, not the humid grip of land, he is the picture of grace, his great weight lightened and moving with stealth and precision. He eats until he is full, darting to the surface occasionally for breath. White surface, black bottom. Telling sounds of fish and calls of other walking whales to either side. The Ambulocetus finds peace in the water.

But as he swims, he has the same dream we all have fifty million years hence: the dream of better versions of ourselves.

He closes his eyes and relaxes his body. His pointed tail, good for balance when he walks but of little use in the water, splits at the end, and each half flattens, so that when his back undulates, his new tail propels him. The burden removed from his hind limbs, they wither. His forelimbs, relieved of their duty to give him stability on the ground, melt into flat appendages like his tail. He need never return to the shore!

He opens his eyes. His senses return to him his long tail and short limbs. He exhales in resignation. Surfaces and breathes. Submerges himself. And dreams.

TERMINAL

The terminals extended from the center of the airport, tentacle-like, delivering passengers to their gates via moving sidewalks, and terminated at jet bridges, where Airbuses and Boeings awaited to take passengers anywhere in the world. The couple's destination was Minneapolis-Saint Paul International and Ellie's mother, who was dying of MS.

They were sitting inside their terminal's Starbucks, drinking coffee to pass the time until they could board. The plan—which was very reasonable—was for Ellie to spend a week relieving her brother from caring for their mother nearly full time. The week would help her decide whether she would return to the coast to finish her PhD or move back home to help with the inevitable. The disease had struck her mother where her limbs terminated, weakening her hands and stiffening her gait; at least, her extremities were where the disease manifested. It had seized control of her nervous system, and as its grip tightened, its damage worked its way inward. Ellie's mother could do nothing but measure the disease's advance and let her children be her hands and feet.

Ellie thought she could be her mother's hands and feet—at least temporarily. There were no Echinoderms in Minnesota. Echinoderms—specifically starfish—were the subject of her PhD. Familiar but beautiful *Asterias rubens*. Slender-armed *Henricia oculata*. Seven-armed *Luidia ciliaris*.

How does one take up starfish as a specialty? She could take the view that it was born in her family's vacations to the Gulf of Mexico, where she and her brother would occasionally see a common starfish swept onto the beach; whoever spotted it would point excitedly, and they would rush toward it as a receding wave snatched it back. More prosaically (because she likely saw more starfish as stiff, dried-out souvenirs in tacky gift shops), there was a progression from a high school biology teacher who saw promise in her to her college major to finding an enjoyable niche for herself in Echinoderm research. It had taken her far from home—and when she went into dissertation mode, and on the job market, she imagined coming home less and less. She already missed her niece and nephew—they were slimmer and longer every time she saw them. But such was life: You outgrew your origins, your younger self.

Simon, whom she had lived with for three years with no sign of a bigger commitment, was coming along to finally meet her family. A conference presentation on mudskippers (of all the fish in the sea) had kept him from accompanying her to her father's funeral. (Fish were his specialty—and he could be so superior about it, just because they were vertebrates!) "If it were *your* father's funeral," she'd said, "I wouldn't skip it for an Echinoderm symposium." "I wouldn't ask you to," he'd said. "*I* don't plan on going to his funeral." He could be so cold. Like a fish. He didn't share her sympathy for her brother. It was his choice to never leave his hometown, Simon had said. And, sure, he spent a lot of time taking care of their mother, but he didn't have to put his life on hold, exactly. "That's what you'd have to do," Simon had warned her. "Would I have to come to Minnesota to see you? You won't be able to go on the job market with me. Be reasonable." Oh, he could be cold. And selfish. She would say his mother would be ashamed of him, but she didn't know his mother. His parents lived within driving distance, but they never visited them. When Ellie became certain that he kept hidden from them the fact that they lived together, she'd said, "What are you, spineless?" He'd stormed out at that. Sometimes she wondered if he really had parents, or if he'd just spawned from the mildewed floors of a lab.

Simon got up and announced that he was taking a walk. He'd not given Ellie time to respond before he was slinking down the concourse, leaving her with their carry-ons. Totally unreasonable! That thought—it was shouted in Ellie's head—brought back his words: "Be reasonable." Be reasonable. It was a mantra with him lately. And that's how she decided she was through with him. She wasn't going to terminate their relationship as they boarded—wasn't going to break up with him on the jet bridge—but she knew this trip would mark the end of it. Be reasonable. She'd grown away from things, but she'd remained tethered, too, held by her pitiful mother, her adorable niece and nephew. Simon was a severed arm, cut off from the past. And he refused to seriously attach himself to her and grow something new. As he walked the concourse, still heading away from her, she realized that he'd never been further from her center than "Be reasonable." He returned when their zone was called. She picked up her carry-on and approached the gate. The image that returned to her as she boarded was that of a common starfish splayed on glistening sand, surprised and pulled by familiar waters back into the ocean.

SON AND HEIR

Rex's feet were swelling in his Nikes, and his eyes burned from the grime that plagued everything. He had driven to the last address he and his ex had for their son and had taken the shoe-leather express from there. At the first apartment, the young man who answered was stoned—it wasn't half past five—and needed his memory jogged to recall Paul ever having lived there. He finally came up with a pink Post-It with an address in Paul's slanted printing. At that address, another young man remembered Paul, and from the troubled look on his face, Rex guessed he'd been pegged as Paul's worried father. This young man produced another address. Rex had underestimated the distance, but he was nearly there now. He wondered if a chorus of young men would keep sending him west until he walked into the Pacific.

If Rex walked with any urgency at all, it was because the evening was getting on and, should he fail in his quest to locate his son (and he was nearly certain he would), he wanted to get back to his own lonely existence before it got too late. There wasn't the urgency of the father who fears his child is in danger; Paul was risk-averse to a fault. Nor was there the urgency of the father who regrets saying something hurtful to his child; there'd been no blowout to precipitate Paul's disappearance. Not that Paul had disappeared, really; he'd faded away. He'd called his father less frequently. Then he'd stopped calling altogether. And stopped taking his father's calls. It was the same with his mother. And it was evident now that he'd stopped sharing his address, too. Rex had set out this evening just to see Paul and say, "I'm here." And wish him a happy birthday.

Rex reached the third apartment at the crest of a hill and, turning east to avoid the sun, removed his glasses and tried rubbing the hurt from his eyes. This time, a young woman opened the door about a third of the way. She kept her shoulders covered with a light shawl. Her ponytail and the sheen of sweat on her cheeks suggested that he'd interrupted her yoga.

"I'm sorry to bother you. Is Paul here? I'm his father."

"Paul? He doesn't live here anymore."

"I'm sorry. But he did live here?"

"Yes. But I don't know where he is now."

The woman seemed older than Paul. Late thirties? She opened the door a touch more; Rex took that softening for pity.

"When did he leave?"

"January? It's been months. Have you tried calling him?"

"He doesn't answer."

The shawl drooped off the woman's shoulders, and she tugged it back up; Rex sensed that her pity was up, and she wanted him to go.

"May I come in?"

"Excuse me?"

"May I come in? I know he's not here, but I'd still appreciate a look around."

"He didn't leave anything behind."

"I'm not looking for anything."

"Good night, then." She went to shut the door, but Rex barred it with his foot.

"Please," he said, "I haven't seen him in a very long time. If you'd just let me inside, I might be able to get… a sense of him. Please?" Rex pulled his foot off the threshold, and the woman opened the door all the way for him.

"Come in."

"Thank you. I'm Rex, by the way."

"Jo."

Rex's airway shrunk ever so slightly. A cat. Would Paul have cared for that? Rex ought to have known. The front room was a loveseat and a couple of chairs, all covered in throws and hugged by potted plants. A yoga mat lay on the hardwood in the center of the room. Straight back was the kitchen and a cloud of turmeric. A hallway on the left surely led to the bedroom and bath.

"Sit down, please," Jo said, sitting in one of the chairs.

Rex sat on the loveseat and searched the room. Paul really didn't leave anything behind. "He really didn't leave anything behind." There were neither esoteric philosophy books nor Jolly Ranchers on the end tables. Paul was deeply into the obscure and occult, but he was also very attached—protective, even—of some of the mass-produced, commercial elements of his youth, especially those hard candies.

"Was it serious?"

Jo laughed. "I don't think he can be serious about anyone but himself."

"I'm sorry. I suppose I'm partly to blame. It's his birthday, you know?" Rex sighed and noticed his strained breathing. He imagined it to be Paul's. If he could properly occupy the space Paul had recently vacated, perhaps he really could get a sense of him. "Did Paul sit here?"

"Other side."

Rex scooted across the loveseat. "And you would've sat here?" He patted the spot he'd just occupied.

Jo nodded.

"Would you sit here?"

"You really miss him?"

"I don't think I realized how much."

Jo let her shawl fall on her chair and joined Rex on the loveseat. Rex could smell her sweat, the same rich stink Paul had once breathed in.

Rex turned to Jo, and she eyed him back; he leaned in, and she leaned out.

"I think you should go."

Rex let himself out.

He faced west, was blinded by the sun, and considered continuing that way, though it was the opposite direction from which he'd come. Paul, leaving Jo's, might've gone that way. Then Rex turned, letting the sun bake his back; of course, Paul could've gone this way, too—and this way led back to his car. This business of trying to walk in his son's shoes was proving unsatisfying, anyway. What Rex wanted was to hold Paul again. So he started walking, an exile scanning the hills for the babe he'd laid aside so long ago.

THE RAGPICKERS AT GETTYSBURG

The Ragpickers learned of the battle from Mr. Pages at the Hauer paper mill in Spring Forge. The three men had been picking rags for him from the farms that dotted the countryside around the village, but with the field hospitals collecting every scrap for bandages, there were no more rags to be had.

"Gettysburg," Mr. Pages had said. "Twenty-four miles west. I don't like the idea one bit, but it's the only chance I've got to keep the mill operating. And you men are nothing but bags of bones."

"You should see our horses," said one of the Ragpickers. "Should we not make it there, we can open a glue factory."

"You'll want to ride by day and pick at night."

"Why's that, sir?"

"They'll be burying the dead all day long, for days, maybe weeks. Look for the unburied."

"We're ragpickers, not graverobbers. Right?"

"Take care to avoid Union eyes," Mr. Pages warned. "And take only rags."

The Ragpickers drove their horses silently, sweltering on the bench seat. York Turnpike was empty save for a wagon being driven out of Gettysburg by a disreputable-looking sort. The wagon driver sneered at them and tightened his grip on his musket, likely stolen from the battlefield, to stave off any attempt by the Ragpickers to rob him. Even if the Ragpickers had wanted to rob him, they had neither the strength nor the guns. The scavenger's wagon, they imagined, was loaded with the arms of the Confederate dead. Maybe Union dead, too. But not rags. So, the Ragpickers nodded gravely and rode on.

Evening came on, and the Ragpickers rode with bowed heads against the setting sun. The drone of crickets in the fields and the clop of hooves was lulling them to sleep. But before they crossed over into slumber, the collapse of one of their horses jerked them to attention. The Ragpickers unhitched the dead horse and dragged her from the road. One of the Ragpickers retrieved a shovel from the wagon.

"You want to bury her?"

"She deserves better than to be left on the side of the road. And we'll build up an enormous appetite."

"You remember we've nothing to eat?"

"Then we'll be ravenous when we finally break our fast. Come on, we'll take turns."

The third Ragpicker took the shovel and broke earth on the shallow grave.

As the Ragpicker who'd proposed the burial laid the last shovelful of dirt onto the grave, he said, "We are *not* doing this again."

Late into the night, the three remaining horses thrashed and snorted, as if afraid to go on. By their lantern light, the Ragpickers could see no more than a few feet in front of their horses, but the death stench told them that they were close to the battlefield.

"We're almost there, girls. Then you can rest."

They crossed Rook Creek and turned south into the death stench. They crested a ridge and arrived at a valley bordered by the creek to the east and a breastwork to the west. Among trees that had been shredded or felled by the battle, massive boulders kept a deathwatch over an untold number of festering bodies stretching before them. Across the valley and over the breastworks, there must have been thousands more. Slaughtered horses, too, picked at by vultures.

The Ragpickers stepped down from the wagon and took a cursory walk among the dead. Union and Confederate, tossed and soiled enough to look like part of the earth. It was horrifying by any measure, but what ultimately unsettled the Ragpickers was the youth of so many of the dead. The Ragpickers' sons would be about the age of these boys. The Ragpickers had not seen their sons in years, but their young, soft faces came to them vividly now.

One of the Ragpickers squatted by an older soldier and took hold of his blue jacket, gently fingering the wool. The soldier appeared to have been stripped of his arms, but the Ragpicker discovered a small sidearm inside his jacket—something overlooked by the scavenger they had passed on the road. He left it on the soldier.

"Let's begin in this valley," he said. "Rags only. Leave everything else."

The Ragpickers grabbed their sacks and systematically worked their way across the valley. With great care, they removed jackets, shirts, trousers, and undergarments. They laid each man's hat across his chest so he could be buried with his Union or Confederate brothers.

The Ragpickers' hands were quickly and deeply stained with blood and earth. When a Ragpicker's sack was full, he slung it over his shoulder and hauled it back to the wagon, emptied it, and began again.

"Come, look!" one of them called.

The others rushed over to see what was the matter, taking care not to trample any of the dead. The first Ragpicker stood and slowly opened his palm to reveal a roll of Necco Wafers.

"I know we're not to take anything but rags…."

"Oh, I doubt the Union will miss these."

So, the Ragpickers divided the wafers and, as they worked into the night, sucked on their chalky sweetness to keep up their spirits.

Until the Union could muster the men to properly attend to the battlefield, the 21st Pennsylvania Cavalry was charged with patrolling the site. They camped just south of Evergreen Cemetery, and though they were nearly starved, rode daily out to the sites of battle east and west to chase away thieves and other curious types, often taking off of them anything they could eat or spend as punishment. Further south, the farms-turned-hospitals were spilling over with injured soldiers; men filled every room of every house and the fields, too. But the sites of battle were generally deserted save the men from town busy digging shallow trenches for unmarked burials.

The morning after the Ragpickers had been at work by Rook Creek, the cavalry had ridden southwest and formed a ring around three boys who'd been spotted among the dead near the hospitals on Taneytown Road. The Captain dismounted and approached the boys. He weaved among the dead and got right up to one of them, who flinched at his yellowed teeth and whiskey breath.

"We were just looking, Captain. Honest."

"Everything in this battlefield is Union property. If I find you've stolen so much as a single Necco Wafer—"

"He's telling the truth, Captain."

The Captain turned to the boy who'd brazenly interrupted him. "You're Widow Wallace's boy, aren't you?"

"Yes, sir."

"I'm disappointed to see you mixed up in this."

"We're sorry, Captain. We won't trespass again."

The Captain said nothing to the boy. "Search them!"

A half-dozen men dismounted and in pairs grabbed the boys and searched them roughly, finding nothing in the boys' pockets but some salted meat, which they took for themselves. The Captain walked over to the widow's boy, who was still held by two of his men. The Captain brought his face very close to the boy's and whispered, "Since you're not helping your poor mother, perhaps you'd like to come back to camp?"

"Thank you, Captain, but she's expecting me back any minute."

"Oh, I doubt she'd mind if you were in the company of a captain of the Union Army."

The Captain removed his gloves. He hooked his fingers into the rim of the boy's trousers, pulling him closer, and the boy tensed in his captors' arms, sickened with fear of what would happen next.

"Captain!" A lone cavalry man was riding in from the east. "Trouble on Culp's Hill!"

The Captain turned toward the voice, and the boys thrashed from the men's holds and ran, dashing across Taneytown Road back to their farms. The Captain huffed at seeing the boys escape, but clearly there was something more pressing than some curious boys. He mounted his horse, and the cavalry rode out to meet the scout.

"What is it, Major?"

"Scores of the dead robbed, Union and Rebel. It's very curious, sir. Many have not been stripped of their arms, but have been desecrated in a rather unusual manner."

"How is that?"

"They've been stripped of their clothes, save their hats."

"Ragpickers. Filthy Irish. Should they come back, we'll make them pay."

Mr. Pages delighted at seeing the Ragpickers' wagon return the next evening, and though he blanched at the blood-stained tears in the uniforms, he paid the Ragpickers well and asked if they would go back for another load. The Rag-pickers, seeing their position, agreed to risk the journey and Union trouble, under certain conditions.

"There is plenty more. You would think a war was being fought! But we'll need to eat first."

"Yes! I'm so hungry, I could eat a horse."

"Though we'd prefer not to; we've already lost one!"

"Certainly," Mr. Pages said. "Allow me to feed you men."

"Our horses, too. Lest they decide to eat us!"

Mr. Pages brought food and beer to the Ragpickers and fed their horses. The Ragpickers ate and drank what they could hold in their shrunken bellies and stuffed their pockets with the leftovers, then slept in the back of their wagon on their empty sacks. They awakened in the morning to the patter of rain on the wagon's roof and again set out for Gettysburg.

Their farmhouse and barn having been turned into a hos-pital overfilled with injured soldiers and the doctors and nurses attending to their wounds, Mrs. Wallace and her son, William, were sitting down in the damp grass behind the house for their supper. The rain had finally stopped, and there was such lovely starlight that for a moment they might forget the calamity that had descended upon them for those three days. They had acclimated to the death stench, and preferred it to the cries of the infected, though those were impossible to escape entirely; nearly all of the men whose beds, as it were, were situated outside of the house and barn, were grievously infected.

As they were saying a prayer, William saw three lights coming over a ridge north of the farm. Lanterns. A wagon, he guessed, from the way they moved. The boy jumped up to take a closer look. Now Mrs. Wallace saw them, too.

"Stay put, son."

"Is it scavengers?"

"It may be. Better go tell the Captain right away."

"The Captain? I thought you wanted me to stay put?"

"Don't be smart, young man."

"Shouldn't I stay here to protect you?"

"No one except the dying wants in here. Maybe not even them. Besides, I've got your father's rifle."

William didn't move. The silence was broken by a moan from one of the fields.

"Hurry up, now."

"They call them the Forty Thieves. They're worse than scavengers."

"What are you talking about? You know what—I don't even want to know. Just get going."

"Yes, ma'am."

William rode up to the cavalry's camp, praying that no one would be there. He didn't like scavengers but would rather see them get away with a few guns and sabers than suffer the Captain's cold fingers on him again. God, he wanted to kill him! If his father were still alive, they would patrol the battlefield, keep it safe from scavengers, and not harass the families that lived there. They would be heroes; the Captain and the Forty Thieves might as well be secesh.

When William arrived at the camp, he found that the cavalry had been joined by a second cavalry, in whose charge were dozens of haggard-looking Confederate prisoners. The prisoners, William came to understand from the captain of the second cavalry, were to be put to work burying the dead.

"And what is your business, young man?" This new captain asked William.

"Scavengers, sir."

"A most unusual thing grows in this valley."

Two nights after their first journey into Gettysburg, the Ragpickers returned to the valley. One of them had his lantern lowered to the earth to show the others what he'd nearly tripped over: From a low mound emerged the toe of a boot. Its partner sprouted next to it.

One of the other Ragpickers bent over and pulled at one of the boots; the earth's grip upon it told him that it remained on its wearer. He might've pulled the boot, foot and all, from the earth, so rotted was the body; instead, he let go. "I suspect this thing has quite the root system."

"We're not graverobbers."

One of the Ragpickers brushed some of the damp earth from the mound and revealed a gray jacket. "This isn't a proper grave." He brushed more earth away, and in a moment a decomposing Confederate soldier lay before them. "So there's nothing to worry about!"

The shallow grave was just one in a long, buried trench that ran parallel to the breastwork. The Ragpickers guessed that a dozen or more soldiers lay there, so that's where they began. After removing a soldier's clothes, they kicked some of the earth back and laid his hat across him.

"How long do you suppose we can go on doing this?"

"Making a killing off dead soldiers? Maybe we'll get lucky and the war will never end!"

After a while, one of the Ragpickers spoke with an earnestness rarely heard among the Ragpickers. "You don't think any of our boys got caught up in this?"

"Not a chance," said one of the others as he was pulling the jacket off a dead soldier. "If they're anything like us, they won't be caught anywhere near this war."

At that moment, the Ragpickers felt the earth quaking as if under a stampede. They turned toward the sound, helplessly.

"Yes," the third Ragpicker said. "Good thing we have more sense than to get involved in the war…."

The cavalry came into view as it rode through a gap in the breastwork and descended into the valley. As the cavalry funneled through, a boy broke off from the line and rode away. The cavalry approached the Ragpickers, and a few men dismounted and immediately climbed into their wagon. The cavalry's leader narrowed his eyes at the Ragpickers, looked at the uncovered and half-stripped bodies at their feet, the soiled sacks in their hands.

"This isn't your first time in Gettysburg, is it, ragpickers?"

"No, sir. Is it yours? Lovely, isn't it?"

The Captain unsheathed his saber and thrust it inches from the Ragpicker's face.

"I've a notion that you've taken arms off the dead."

"We've not taken anything but rags, sir."

One of the men called from the wagon, "Nothing but clothes here, sir."

"See?" said the Ragpicker. "Holey things, too. And bloody, very bloody. Beyond mending."

"Shut up!" yelled the Captain. "Search them."

Men grabbed the Ragpickers and emptied their pockets of salted meat, crusts of bread, and the last few Necco Wafers.

"For the unholy crime of desecrating the bodies of Union soldiers, men who gave their lives to preserve these United States, you degenerate Irish ragpickers are sentenced to burn the bodies of all the fallen horses in this valley."

"There must be hundreds," said one of the Ragpickers. "Any chance we could get back those wafers, sir? It would make for much quicker work."

The Captain crushed the candies in his fist.

"On second thought, why don't you enjoy them? They do something wonderful for your disposition."

The Ragpickers, along with the prisoners, began dragging the picked-at horses toward the center of the valley for burning. Some horses were intact and required several men to move. Others, whose joints had been chewed by animals, were in pieces that a single man could carry. The Ragpickers couldn't decide which was worse. A cavalry man lighted the pile of rotting flesh.

"At least," said one of the Ragpickers, "we don't have to bury them."

As dawn approached, and with it more rainfall, the cavalry and the prisoners watched the pile smolder. The reek reignited the olfactories of the cavalry and the prisoners, who'd grown used to the death stench. Mrs. Wallace and William and the doctors and nurses and suffering men housed at their farm were overtaken by it, too.

And the Ragpickers laughed.

CHAMP

Evan Johns Youth Baseball Camps ran for one week at each Little League they visited. Evan gave no more instruction than any of the other half-dozen ex-ballplayers on staff—career minor leaguers who'd never been called up to the Big Show long enough to have a baseball card printed—but he'd played a few seasons in the majors and delivered a crucial pinch hit in a League Championship game, so his was the name and face of the venture. He gave opening remarks and coached hitting and infielding to the Little Leaguers that were dropped off each morning, divided up for drills, served lunch in the nearby pavilions, then sorted into teams for scrimmages. After five days, the kids went home with a baseball autographed by the ex-pros, and the ex-pros moved on to the next Little League.

The Little Leaguers gathering for this camp were still dragging in from the parking lot, some carrying duffels and others with their bats slung on their shoulders and their gloves threaded around the ends like hobo bags. It wasn't even 9 a.m. and the humidity was suffocating. They checked in and put on their Evan Johns Youth Baseball Camps LLC t-shirts.

In the parking lot, a woman in yoga pants and enormous sunglasses ruffled her son's cap.

"You ready, Champ?"

"I don't see why I have to miss the tournament for this."

"Because you need to play sports, not just card games. Now make the best of it."

She went to kiss him, which sent him flying toward the check-in area.

"I love you," she called. "Listen to your coaches."

After checking in, the boy, Nate, sat in right field with the other kids. The coaches stood around talking in grown-up voices. Then Coach Johns gave something like a pep talk. His remarks were brief, rehearsed: Open batting stance. Soft hands.

Nate was in Coach Johns' infielding group that morning. Coach Johns spoke to his group about fundamentals, modeled some techniques, then set a few kids at each position to take turns fielding grounders. There was the steady rhythm of the ball pinging off Coach Johns' bat, thumping the infield dirt, then smacking into the first basemen's glove. Over this, Coach Johns repeated "Soft hands" like a mantra. After a while, he called them in for a water break. The kids pulled bottled waters from a cooler and sat behind home plate.

Coach Johns removed his cap and wiped away sweat with his forearm.

"It's hotter than hell out here. Good thing I got my summer haircut."

The swearing and the joke about his baldness warmed the kids to him. Then he could talk to his groups, find out who were teammates or rivals in the Little League, who were the entitled coaches' sons.

"What about you?" He nodded toward Nate, who was drawing in the dirt with his finger.

"I don't know."

"Got a favorite team?"

"I don't know."

"Favorite player?"

"I don't know."

"Are you sure you're at the right camp?" Evan forced a laugh as he said this.

One of the boys said, "God, you're gay," and the other kids laughed uncomfortably.

"That's enough," Evan snapped. He turned his gaze on the boy who'd said it. "You, go run the perimeter of the field. Move it!"

Evan turned back to Nate.

"Sorry, Kid. You were doing a great job at second, by the way."

It was the end of the third day, and all the kids had been picked up except Nate. The ex-pros, except for Coach Johns, were standing around the full-size van they traveled in, eager for the last one to be picked up so they could head back to their hotel and dinner. Coach Johns was in the infield, talking on his phone.

After a few minutes, he walked over to the bleachers where Nate was waiting.

"Hey, Nate. Your mom called. Something came up at work and she can't get you."

"She's stuck at the gym? That's never happened."

"Well, it happened today."

"How am I going to get home?"

"That's the cool part. Hop in the van. I'll take you home."

Nate followed Coach Johns to the van. None of the other ex-pros said anything when Nate climbed into the front passenger seat and laid his bat and glove on the floor. Coach Johns hopped into the driver's seat and started the engine.

"So, Nate, do you feel like you're getting a lot out of the camp? Anything you really want to work on?"

"It's fine."

"You're really improving in the infield."

"I suck at hitting."

"You're putting the ball in play. A little. We'll get you there, right, Tommy?" Coach Johns smiled in the rearview at one of the ex-pros, who gave no reply.

"But you're enjoying yourself?" Coach Johns asked, quietly. "Sometimes you look like you'd rather be someplace else."

"Sort of. My mom made me come."

"Really?"

"But it's okay."

"'It's okay.' Terrific."

"Nate, Mr. Johns has asked us to have dinner with him tonight."

"What?"

It was the close of the fourth day, and Nate had just gotten into his mother's car.

"He'd like to take us to dinner."

"When?"

"Tonight."

"Why?"

"He must like you."

"But isn't it weird?"

"Coach Johns is obviously taking an interest in you. Give him a chance."

"A chance to what?"

"Talk to you. About baseball. Anything."

Nate and his mother met Coach Johns at Ponderosa. They sat in a booth, Nate next to his mother and Coach Johns across from them. Nate's mother sent him to the buffet.

"Is this okay?" Evan asked. "I would've liked to take you someplace nicer, but things have been tight since the divorce."

"This is fine."

"You look nice, Allison."

"Please. I just threw this on."

"I think Nate's terrific." Evan smiled deprecatingly. "I don't think he cares much about baseball, but he seems to be a really great kid."

"Yeah. He's into video games, stuff like that. The other night he told me he wanted to join a live-action role playing club."

"What's that?"

"It's where they dress up and play Dungeons and Dragons or whatever."

"Huh."

"At least they're running around outside instead of sitting on their butts in some kid's basement."

They laughed, not noticing that Nate was returning. He slid into the booth and stuck a chicken wing in his mouth. Their steaks were delivered, and for a few moments, they ate quietly.

"So, Nate, your mom tells me you're into some kind of dress-up game. What's that like?"

"Mom!"

"Sorry. We were talking."

"What else did you talk about?"

Allison and Evan looked at each other, unsure how to answer.

"Coach, do you have kids?"

"I was married. But we didn't have children."

"My mom never was married, but she had me. That's funny. Excuse me."

Nate slid out of the booth and walked toward the restrooms.

On the last day of camp, Nate went through the drills with no more or less enthusiasm than he had the first four days. For the final scrimmage, Nate was placed on Coach Johns' team and slated to start at second base and bat sixth. It was baldly preferential. They batted first. Two batters made it on base; the fifth batter went down swinging for the third out, leaving Nate on deck.

Nate returned to the bench. When the team took the field, he stayed put, his glove in the dirt at his feet.

"Nate," Coach Johns said. "Why aren't you out there?"

"I'm not feeling well. I'd like to go home now."

"Are you sure? You're going to miss all the end-of-camp fun. There's going to be ice cream."

"Will you call my mom?"

Nate had understood the deception since he'd returned from the buffet. He didn't enjoy his food. He went straight to his room and lay in bed, imagining what he might say to his mother, what she might say back. Imagining, too, what might happen between her and that man. He'd finally fallen asleep in his clothes and been woken up by his mother, standing in his door saying, "You okay, Champ?" as if nothing had happened. As if she hadn't turned their whole world upside down.

When she arrived at the Little League, she waited until they were out of sight of the kids and the ex-pros and Evan before holding him in her arms.

"I'm sorry, Champ."

LONGBOXES OF LOVE

He was a conscientious B-student and trusted office aide, which was how he found himself responsible for restocking the Coke and snack machines during sixth period. He took the keys from the office, opened the machines, marked on a scrap of paper how many Cokes and Sprites and Snickers, etc. were needed from the stock room, then brought the drink and snack cases out on a dolly and readied the machines for the day's extracurriculars: basketball practice, cheer, maybe a dance he wouldn't go to. The final step was emptying the machines of the flattened ones and fives. He stuffed these greasy green stacks into a blue bank-deposit bag and returned it and the keys to the office. The paper on which he recorded what was removed from the stock room was folded up in his pocket to be discarded later.

After school he rode the bus home and did his homework, the little TV in his room tuned, as always, to MTV. There was *Yo! MTV Raps* in the afternoon and *Headbangers Ball* and—his favorite—*120 Minutes*, at night. Somewhere in this period he earned his permit and was occasionally asked by his mother to run into town for something or other from Wal-Mart, and he'd use the opportunity to spend a few precious minutes in Ear-X-Tacy, browsing the Alternative section's CD longboxes. Though it was only half the size of an LP sleeve, for someone born too late to have ever owned an LP, the CD longbox afforded a pleasing visual on the front and a track listing and maybe a second image on the back. Some were works of art! Jane's Addiction's *Ritual de lo habitual*! Pray, what wonders besides the track he'd seen/heard on *120 Minutes* did this CD hold? But he had nothing to put in Ear-X-Tacy's coffers!

That's when he began skimming from the vending machine deposits. He started by swiping a five; he could always say he must have dropped it. The next day, nothing was said to him, so he took a handful of ones. Again, no one noticed. With the skimmed cash he bought Nirvana's *Nevermind*. The longbox seemed to shimmer in his hand, what with the water all down its front side. He brought it home, gently removed it from its longbox, inserted it in the living room stereo, and listened to it in headphones straight through, twice. Yes, the entire album, *twice*; it sustained him!

Pause, Reader of Today, and imagine yourself as a teenager in suburbia in 1992, oblivious to the ease with which you would one day leisurely pull up videos on your smartphone and download songs, by means legal or otherwise, in mere seconds. Our boy in 1992 humbled himself before the altar of MTV to receive three-minute visions from musical prophets: St. Cornell. The Goddess PJ Harvey. Morrissey the Celibate. Rollins, High Priest of Loneliness. And the Messiah: Cobain. And when their missives came, all else be damned, you had to pay attention.

Our boy absorbed their missives and felt called to study their sacred texts known as albums, to hear the deep tracks and CD bonus cuts, to be a true disciple of the prophets. This is how he found himself listening to an ill-gotten Nirvana CD on a winter's day in the Year of our Lord 1992. He skimmed more and bought more CDs and taped the longboxes to the walls of his room, and in his temple he lay ruining his hearing with the Discman he'd bought, also with skimmed money.

All of this is preface; what's important is what he did with his riches that spring (and it was riches; between lunch periods and practices and games, no one was going 'round hungry). In the freak kids at the back of the bus, he recognized the moshers in the Nirvana and Sonic Youth videos. He'd always sat in a no-man's land between the debauched back rows and the straights at the front of the bus, positioned so he could hear the dirty jokes, which he sometimes was brave enough to turn around and laugh at, cautiously stepping into the freaks' turf. When he got the Discman, he started listening to it on the bus in the hopes that one of them would tap him on the shoulder and ask what he was playing. Maybe the clean-cut one who told the filthiest jokes would ask and, being duly impressed that it was *Bleach*, sponsor him into the group. But when the tap came, it was the red-headed wispy-mustached ringleader, and all he said was, "Lemme listen." Was his Discman getting stolen? Oh, irony! No, the ringleader just wanted a listen. After one track he gave it back and said, "Whaddaya think, is it as good as *Nevermind*?" "You wanna borrow it and see?" Then our boy had a thought that made itself into speech before he could check it: "Go ahead. You can have it." "Really?" "Yeah." The rest of the gang got interested. "I've been getting these for nothing, really," he said. "I empty the vending machines at school, and I keep a little of the money each day. Nobody notices. It's like the basketball team and drama club are paying for these." He flashed them a few other CDs that were tucked in his backpack." "Well," said the clean-cut one, "I buy a Coke and some Captain's Wafers every day, so where's mine?"

So, he started skimming a little more and buying more CDs, and at least once a week on the morning bus ride, he'd open his backpack to pull out a half-dozen longboxes, a brick of alternative rock. The ringleader grabbed them from his hand to take first pick. "I LOVE THESE LONGBOXES!"

He was now one of the freak kids at the back of the bus, which meant trading jokes and barbs and talking new videos and deep tracks every morning and afternoon for half-an-hour and saying "eat shit" to the rest of the gang when it was your stop. The Friday before spring break, since none of them were headed to sunnier places, he was told they were round-robining at each other's houses and he should join them. So, he rode his bike to one of their houses each afternoon, where they listened to CDs while playing Super Nintendo, ashed cigarettes into empty Coke cans, and talked about girls. He hosted, too, supplying his freak friends with endless Cokes and chips. His longbox temple was full of parishioners, and he felt blessed and thanked his prophets and the fortunes of the vending machines.

Being away from the routine of the machines, however, allowed a niggling worry to grow—a worry that his luck was about to give, that someone had finally done some accounting and would finger him at any moment. But when he returned, he wasn't pulled from Biology to an interrogation. Still, he was reticent to skim even a dollar for the first couple of weeks back. His friends started asking when their next longbox was coming.

So, he started skimming again, but afraid of being noticed—surely the discrepancy would catch someone's attention—he supplemented with an occasional bill or two lifted from his mother's wallet. Still, he made fewer gifts to his freak friends, and explained away the slowdown in production by saying that some of the new stuff coming out just wasn't worth it. Sellouts.

In this way, he made it to the end of the year. And was never caught! His gifts of longboxes did not earn him any contact with the freak kids that summer, which was disappointing, but his time with them had loosened him up a bit, and junior year he made new friends and didn't spend so much time on his own, in front of MTV, though he stayed tuned for new missives from the alternative rock prophets.

This is still preface, perhaps: Our boy survived high school, spent four uneventful years at a state school, got married, had a son whom he didn't spend as much time with as he would've liked (all very "Cat's in the Cradle") before his divorce, and now saw even less. He was at Wal-Mart choosing something for his son's seventh birthday. He picked up a set of Legos and had to catch his breath; the long, rectangular box in his hand telescoped a sensation from a quarter-century ago: a half dozen CD longboxes about to be paid to the freak kids for their friendship. Was he doing it again? Was he buying his kid's love? He was!

His ex's protests be damned! He would go to his kid's birthday party. A boy needs his father. Everyone knows that.

He bought the Legos anyway. No sense in punishing the child for the sins of the father.

BACKHANDED COMPLIMENTS AND ONE-NIGHT STANDS

There's two men sitting in a booth drinking Budweiser and eating baskets of greasy fries, when something that never happens happens: Two women ask if they can join them. Of course, these homely men say okay, and the women remove their hats and coats, and introductions are made. When everything's settled, it's clear that the women have made pairs of them, and one of the men is all grins about this. His buddy is still brooding about getting dumped, though the grinning man thinks it was long enough ago and with enough force that he ought to move on.

The grinning man just about loses it when the woman next to him brings her face close to his and he smells her bready cheeks. It's love at first smell! She works at the university. Office stuff. Very boring. But she writes poetry. Just some things in little journals. Nothing really.

While the grinning man is falling for the bready poet, his brooding buddy is looking for a way out. The woman who's chosen him has enormous gums, like a mile of gums between her upper lip and her front teeth, which are nothing to sneeze at, either. She talks to him, and when her gums dry out, she washes them with her tongue. He's a bad conversation partner, but she keeps talking, working her whole excited mouth.

There's more drinking. When the grinning man can think of nothing to say into the bready poet's mouth, and his brooding buddy can't be drawn out anymore, the women talk to each other, laugh at private jokes, then excuse themselves for the ladies' room.

The grinning man tells his brooding buddy, "Thanks for putting up with her friend. I think there might be something with this one!"

"Whatever."

"For someone so totally thoughtless and self-centered, it's very considerate of you."

The women return and grab their hats and coats and say they've had a nice time. The bready poet slides her number to the grinning man. Then they're gone.

This is when the brooding man realizes his mistake. He let a rare chance for the affection of another human being escape him. He tries desperately to recall features of the woman's face besides her enormous gums, but can't.

As the men are about to leave, the women come back in from the cold. The woman with the enormous gums has locked her keys in her car. The brooding man is awestruck: green eyes, bent nose, and that shiny pink gumscape that seems to him a gift. The grinning man elbows him and says to stop standing there and come help.

The men step out onto the sidewalk. The grinning man finds a wire coat hanger among the take-out cups and receipts and CDs on his backseat, while the awestruck man finds the hatchback they're to break into. The grinning man returns and, grinning at passersby to show that everything's on the level, skillfully unlocks the car.

When they return to the booth, the women have bought them more drinks. How did you do that! they wonder. Before the grinning man can speak, his buddy is describing to his green-eyed crush how he shaped a tool from an ordinary hanger and unlocked her car without doing any harm to it. It requires a certain touch, he says, splaying his beefy hands in front of her. This gross display, so at odds with the subtleness described in his false account of unlocking the car, screws up the grin on his friend's face. But his friend doesn't contradict the story.

By last call, it's understood that the pairs are going home together. Before they part, the awestruck man says to his friend, "Thanks for letting me take all the credit back there!"

"No problem."

"Given your fragile sense of self and insatiable need to please everyone, that was awfully humble of you."

The pairs find themselves in separate rooms. Lights are dimmed, stereos are turned on, and drinks are poured. A continuation of the bar, of the shedding of self-consciousness that can occur only under cover of music and laughter and the clinking of ice in tumblers. Eventually, each yields to their partner. The music stops. The only sounds are the whispers they make against each other. Those whispers say: Thank you for not leaving me alone tonight. For someone driven into the arms of a stranger to seek a reprieve from crushing loneliness and self-doubt, your presence is a gift. It is an act of kindness.

ELI'S TROUBLE

Eli Katz was showing the new guy, Bruce, the engine of a Chevy pickup. Eli's hands were grease-smudged all the way to his wrists where the blue edges of his full sleeves began. Bruce's hands were in his pockets. As Eli identified the engine's components, he sensed his words ricocheting off the kid's flat face. Starter. Bounce. Alternator. Bounce. Intake manifold. Bounce, bounce. Their boss, Dave, had told Eli only yesterday morning that Bruce, who was soon to be Dave's son-in-law, would be joining them at the garage. He promised Eli it wouldn't affect his pay or hours, but he needed help getting Bruce trained since Bruce had never done this kind of work. The last thing Dave said about it was, "This wasn't my idea."

Eli didn't like this news. He'd just started feeling something like happiness. He'd been happy before, for sure: as a child playing on the sloping lawn between his house and the neighbors', competing in cross country in high school—even as late as his thirtieth birthday last summer when he and T.S. spent the weekend in Tunica, leaving the Texas hold 'em tables only to refuel at the buffet and make a Kenny Rogers show just to get drunk at the bar until he sang "The Gambler." But those things were all fleeting. Now Eli's life seemed happily settled. Since Dave's only other employee had left last fall—and thank God, that dope was a waste of space always going on about his bratty kids—it was just

Dave and Eli in the garage. It felt like a family business; the garage backed up to the rear of the bungalow Dave bought after his divorce, and Eli and Dave ate lunch in Dave's kitchen, Eli freely rummaging in the fridge for cold cuts and sodas. Eli's actual father was an American Airlines pilot. Something about commanding a jet and seeing all those different cities, banging flight attendants—and he did wonder about his father's fidelity—used to appeal to Eli, but it failed to excite him anymore. He was happy in the garage, removing what was worn and broken in an engine and replacing it with solid new parts, like surgery, and he enjoyed doing it with Dave. And there was Laurie, the first girl he'd ever been serious about. No more picking up girls at the bars.

To say he'd arrived at this happy state isn't quite right; it would be better to say he was rudely delivered there one night last month at the Brew Co. T.S.'s band, Group Sex, was grinding out the punk anthems he and Eli had grown up with, stuff by Black Flag, Circle Jerks, Dead Kennedys. T.S., with his mushroom cloud of curls adding even more height to his six feet, towered over the kids drawn to the stage to slam or whatever they were calling it now. Eli and the others who'd outgrown all that crowded in the back. Laurie wasn't there, so Eli was a bit drunk. When a bony-faced guy sidled up to him and said, "You're Eli Katz," Eli said, "And you're fucking annoying." The jerk's hard cheeks and pointed noise weren't familiar, but maybe Eli had seen him before—his whole goddamned generation looked the same to him: the same teased hair on guys and girls (his own hair was like wool), the same aloof look that sometimes made him think the only thing that ever got any of them off was other people's misery. The jerk didn't look like he was going to shove off. Then a hot pain flared in Eli's side, and a cold sweat shot from his temples down his spine. He reached for the hot spot in his side and found the jerk's girlish fingers wrapped around the hilt of a knife. Eli pulled the knife out, and his cold sweat pooled in his feet, unsteadying him, but the fear of another strike made him hold on. People screamed and pushed themselves away from the struggle, and the jerk yelled something at Eli as he tried freeing the knife. Finally, it popped from Eli's hands like a cork and slashed the cheek of a girl trying to escape, reducing her cries to a pained moan as she went to her knees and pressed her palm against the gash. Eli remembered seeing blood drip through her fingers, some guys making enough sense of the scene to tackle the jerk, and then passing out.

At the hospital, Eli was told he was lucky: The knife didn't damage any major organs. He didn't want to stay overnight, but his father insisted on him staying there until he could get in from O'Hare. Eli's mother came for a while and kissed him goodnight. A moment later, a girl stepped into the dim light of his room. Not Laurie—T.S. had promised not to tell Laurie, Eli would explain it to her tomorrow. It was the girl from the show. A white bandage stretched from one corner of her lips across her cheek and under her blond bob.

"I just wanted to see how you were," she said.

"I'm alive."

"Why was that guy trying to kill you?"

"He yelled something about me and his girlfriend."

"Was it true?"

Eli had laid a lot of girls, but it wasn't his style to get involved—even for a night—with one who was spoken for. But sometimes girls didn't tell.

Eli shrugged. "How're you?"

The girl touched the bandage.

"I'm going to have a scar," she said, starting to cry.

"I'm sorry."

After the stabbing, Eli was happy to spend his evenings in with Laurie. But after about a week, he grew restless, and they started going out again. It was exciting to tell the story, and Laurie didn't mind that when his audience asked him why the jerk had done it, he answered, "Guy thought I'd laid his girlfriend. It's not my fault she was out looking for something better." Laurie could laugh because Eli had assured her that those days were behind him.

But they weren't that far behind: The last girl he'd picked up before meeting Laurie was Krystal Payne, Dave's daughter. He'd met her only once at the garage, and on this Saturday night didn't recognize her. Strands of reddish-blond whorled around her face, bunched in her turtleneck, and he imagined these strands as never ending; if he stripped her, he'd find her body woven in this silk. He'd bought her two drinks before she told him who she was ("Your boss is my dad, you doofus!"), but by that time he'd already decided he wanted to see all that silk. And he did, knowing the whole time he wouldn't see her again; too messy getting involved with the boss's daughter. Monday, working next to Dave, their greased fingers touching as they exchanged parts, he felt sick with himself. If he'd fuck over his boss's daughter, who wouldn't he fuck over? But it seemed he'd gotten away with it. Then last week, Dave announced that Krystal was marrying her boyfriend.

"Who's her boyfriend?" Eli had asked.

"Some kid named Bruce. Only been seeing him a few months."

"That's fast."

"It's a *shotgun wedding*."

Krystal was nine weeks along. That, and Eli's having forgone a condom (if a girl didn't ask for one of the goddamn things, he assumed she was on the pill), told him he had at least a fifty percent chance of being the one the shotgun ought to be pointed toward. After that, things fell like dominos: Dave's ex-wife forced him to take Bruce on at the garage (the kid was working in a comic book shop, for God's sake), and since Dave wasn't too cool on the kid yet, Eli would be responsible for teaching him everything, and since the kid was going to be working at the garage, Eli expected Krystal to start showing up every goddamn day. When Bruce showed up Friday morning, Eli felt the same cold sweat roll down his back and into his feet as he'd felt when he was stabbed.

After Eli had shown Bruce the Chevy's engine, they went after a new fuel pump. Eli drove, hanging his arm out of Dave's pickup's window to get tickled by the sun. The sweet scent of dogwoods, bursting pink and white throughout Tyler Park, softened the iron smell in Eli's nose. He loved running for a part on a day like this, only today he had Bruce to deal with. The kid sat there picking at his greaseless nails looking embarrassed, like he'd fallen for some elaborate joke. When Eli heard Krystal was marrying her boyfriend when her baby might not even belong to him, he figured that if the guy didn't have enough backbone to say he didn't want to play daddy, he was getting what he deserved. But Eli hadn't been imagining Bruce at the time. Bruce was just a kid—a soft twenty-two-years old. The shoulder-length hair and small frame gave Eli the impression of a little girl. It wasn't right, this kid getting trapped like this.

"When's the wedding?" Eli asked.

"Not till October. She and her mother are Catholic, and you've got to be engaged for at least six months for a Catholic wedding."

"You excited?" Hell, if the kid was excited, Eli could just let it go. No one would ever know the baby's real father, not even Krystal. Though maybe she'd be able to see it. What if *everyone* could see it? What if it came out with a woolly head like his own? Maybe it would never see the light of day—a lot can go wrong. The kid was mumbling something Eli hadn't caught the beginning of.

"It's unexpected, you know?" Bruce was saying. "I'm still getting used to the idea."

"Is it what you want to do? Get married to this girl?"

"I guess. I don't know. We love each other, but we hadn't talked about marriage or anything. It seemed too soon."

"How come she didn't take care of it?"

"She wouldn't do that. I wouldn't want her to, anyway."

"Why don't you wait, then? Move in together, have the baby, see how it goes."

Bruce shook his head no. "Krystal and her mother would never go for that."

"Well, you should have a say, too," Eli said, getting indignant, wanting to protect the kid. "That's what's so unfair about this kind of situation: The girl has all the power. She wants to get rid of it, she can get rid of it. She wants to have it and make you pay for it for the rest of your life, she can do that. It just pisses me off."

"Well, I don't see what I can do about it," Bruce said. "Besides, it's mine, too. That's the crazy part—we were so careful. I wore a condom *every* time."

"Was she not taking the pill?"

"No."

So that was it. Eli's chance of being the father just shot up to ninety-nine percent.

"She said she couldn't enjoy it when she was on the pill."

"Well, let her see how she enjoys squeezing out that bastard."

"It won't be a *bastard*," Bruce said.

"I'm sorry," Eli said. "I just hate to see a kid like you getting trapped like this. Especially you."

When Eli and Bruce got back to the garage, Krystal was there. Her reddish-blond silk was tied in a bun, and she was wearing her cosmetology school white blouse and black pants. She was sitting in Dave's chair, cradling a Wendy's bag. Though Eli had expected her, he hadn't worked out the best way of handling her.

"I brought you boys lunch," she said.

Bruce walked over and kissed her cheek. When she handed him his burger, he unwrapped its silver paper on a neat stack of work orders on Dave's desk, then dumped out his fries, letting the grease soak through the wrapping and into the work orders. He had no respect for this business. But at twenty-two Eli hadn't had respect for much either, so it didn't change the fact that he hated to see the kid's life ruined.

Krystal held out a burger for Eli. When he hesitated, she smiled and said, "Well, come on. I'm not going to bring it to you." She was at ease around him, but she was the more skilled at lies and half-truths and cover-ups, so why shouldn't she be?

"I didn't know what you liked on yours, so I got you everything," she said. "Bruce is such a baby he won't get anything on his. How's he doing on his first day?"

"Fine."

Then she said to Bruce, "Dad says he invited you to the guys' jam session tonight."

Oh, Christ. That was the first Eli had heard of this. Bruce said nothing, just chewed with his mouth slightly open.

"I've got to get going," Krystal said. "You boys have a good afternoon."

As she stood, Bruce swallowed and moved toward her for a goodbye kiss, but she didn't notice and walked out the bay door to her car, leaving Bruce standing there with that same embarrassed look he'd had in the pickup. Eli swallowed his last bite and crumpled his silver paper into a ball. He shot it toward the garbage can in the corner, where it bounced off the rim and landed at Bruce's feet.

Monday morning, Bruce stepped on the edge of a full oil pan, sending the grainy slick from a Volvo wagon all over his shoes. He and Eli used every last clean rag sopping up the spill while Dave searched his house for an old pair of shoes to lend Bruce for the rest of the day. When Bruce stuck his feet into some old Converse that were at least a size too big, Dave said, "You look like a clown." Bruce accepted the comment with his stony little-girl look. The kid did nothing so bad for the rest of the week, though he did nothing especially well either. His incompetence wouldn't have been so bad if he'd shown some enthusiasm about the work. But he was just as stone-faced when a job was finished, and Eli prompted him by rubbing his hands together and saying, "All done" or "Nice work," as he was when he'd stepped into that oil pan.

Eli was spared any more visits from Krystal. He figured Bruce had forgotten all about their talk in the pickup last week, and that the wedding was going forward as planned. He was assured of this during lunch on Friday when he found Bruce reading a pamphlet titled FOUNDATION FOR MARRIAGE. They were sitting at the edge of the bay on buckets, letting the sun warm them. Dave was inside; his ex-wife had been calling him every day around noon, and Dave carried the phone inside and ate his lunch while—at least this is what Eli suspected—he gave her an update on Bruce. This left Eli and Bruce eating their lunches on these buckets, not saying much to each other.

"By the way," Bruce said, "I won't be able to hang out with you guys tonight."

Every Friday night, after he went home and showered, Eli picked up T.S. and came back to Dave's, where the three of them stomped down the basement stairs and cranked out classic rock covers, mostly Van Halen and AC/DC, Dave wailing on his Les Paul, Eli pounding his drums, and T.S. thumping his bass and singing everything in his raspy pot-smoker's voice. Last week, in an effort to make his future son-in-law feel welcome, Dave had invited Bruce to join them, even though the kid knew nothing about music. Dave's idea was to let him try out the bass, so T.S. could concentrate on vocals (this hardly mattered). T.S. draped his bass over Bruce's shoulder and gave him a quick lesson. "What do a stripper and a guitar have in common?" he asked. Bruce shrugged. "A *G* string!" T.S. said, popping the bass's thinnest string. They tried "Ain't Talkin' 'Bout Love," with its repeating bass riff, but Bruce wasn't getting it, and the bottom end fell out. He didn't even seem to enjoy it that much.

"That's a shame," Eli said.

"I have to go with Krystal to this thing," Bruce said, holding his pamphlet out for Eli.

Eli didn't want to touch the thing; the life described in it was nothing like his own. He didn't have any need for religion or marriage. But he couldn't just let the thing hang there, so he took it and opened it. From a glance, he understood FOUNDATION FOR MARRIAGE to be like camp. There was a list of topics to be covered: Marriage as a Sacrament, Communication, Budgeting as a Couple, Christian Sexuality, and Family of Origin.

"Jesus, kid, they're covering everything," he said, handing back the pamphlet. "Good luck getting all your badges."

"It's not a big deal."

"Sorry about what I said last week. That stuff about you getting trapped."

"It's okay."

"I wasn't saying you ought to break it off or anything. It might be what I'd do in your situation, but that's just me. You know what you want to do."

That night, while Bruce was at marriage camp, Eli, T.S., and Dave rejuvenated their set; order was restored to the basement. Around ten, Eli and T.S. drove to Eli's house, a little bungalow only a few minutes from Dave's. Eli recognized the rusty Ford Festiva they pulled behind, but not from his street. Where'd he seen this toy of a car? As Eli passed the car on the way to his front door, the shadows revealed someone in the driver's seat—a girl with dark hair. Her face turned toward him. It was Bruce.

"What in the hell are you doing here?" Eli asked.

"You were right," Bruce answered, getting out of his tiny car. "I don't have to marry Krystal just because she's pregnant. We don't even have to stay together if we don't want to."

Eli's luck had just run out. "Did something happen at marriage camp?"

"I blew it off."

"What?"

"I blew it off. I got ready and was about to leave to pick up Krystal when I realized that my whole life was going to change because of this one thing, and I just thought, Eli's right, I don't have to get trapped by this. So I came here instead. I thought I could hang out with you guys tonight."

"How long have you been sitting here?"

"Since eight. The retreat started at six, but I got some Arby's and then went to the comic book shop for a while." On the passenger seat were a paper bag, an X-Men comic, and the tie he'd apparently been wearing before deciding to make his break.

"Really? Maybe you'd better come inside."

"It's not like your life isn't going to change at all," T.S. said. "You're going to have to pay child support, right? And just because you're not with the girl doesn't mean you're not the kid's dad. Shit, my parents have hated each other's guts since I was five, but my dad's still my dad, you know?"

Eli, T.S., and Bruce had slid into a booth at the Brew Co. and ordered a round of beers. There was no band tonight, only the jukebox and the usual pack for them to talk over: men in short-sleeved pearl-button shirts (like Eli and T.S. had) and women in short skirts or tight jeans and flowing tunics. Eli was glad Bruce was getting out of his engagement to Krystal—it would spare the kid a life of misery and deflect some of the guilt he was feeling over letting the kid believe he was the father—but he wasn't thrilled by the way he'd done it. It was too dramatic; surely Krystal and her mother were out for the kid's blood. Dave wasn't going to like it either. Everyone getting excited over Bruce's trick just made Eli more afraid that the truth would come out. Eli also wasn't pleased with the direction T.S. had taken the conversation. Child support. Was there a way Eli could help Bruce out with that without letting him know the truth? And Jesus, where was T.S. going with all that "dad" business? Bruce wasn't going to be anyone's dad—he was still a kid himself.

"That's fine, I'll help raise it," Bruce said. "I was thinking it might be kind of cool to have a boy."

"Fuck that," Eli said. "You're not going to be anyone's dad. Krystal's going to squeeze that thing out, then when she gets her looks back she'll bag some other sucker, and he'll be its dad." That's it—Eli's bastard would be a gift to someone. He could live with that.

"I'll still be involved, won't I?"

"Why is this such a big deal to you?" Eli asked. "I think you've proved tonight that you *don't* want to be involved."

"Maybe I shouldn't have done that," Bruce said. "What do you think I should do?"

"Just tell her as soon as possible," Eli said. "Things ought to play out just like I said."

"I don't know," T.S. said. "I've never knocked anyone up that I know of, but I think if I did I'd have to be part of the kid's life. Starting with watching the girl get all pregnant. And then being there for the birth? That's got to be pretty amazing. Like, there's a sweaty woman yelling at you, then all of a sudden there's a new person—there's life. You've just *made life*."

Eli swallowed the last of his beer and set the bottle down hard. "Why don't you just shut up?"

T.S. asked what Eli's problem was, but Eli didn't answer because he was straining to see a flash of color among all the dark tones at the bar: a girl in a long, pale-green skirt and a short, pink cardigan, topped with reddish-blond silk.

"There she is," Eli said.

Bruce turned around, then quickly turned back to hide his face. "What should I do?"

"That's her?" T.S. asked. "Nice. She doesn't look pregnant."

Having gotten her drink, Krystal was headed toward their booth.

"Eli, what do I do?"

"I think we've got to play this one by ear."

Krystal slid into the booth next to Bruce. For all the trouble she was in, being knocked up by one guy and tenuously engaged to another, she pulled off an amused smile as she said to him, "I didn't expect to find you here."

"Then why'd you come here? And what are you drinking? You're not supposed to drink."

"See," T.S. said, bringing that side of the table into what Eli hoped would be a negotiation, some working out of things, between only Bruce and Krystal, "He's already acting like a dad. 'What are you drinking? You shouldn't be drinking.'"

"Relax—it's a Diet Coke," Krystal said. "Anyway, I waited for you for an hour. When I couldn't get you on your cell and your parents didn't know where you were, I figured you were having second thoughts and had gone off somewhere to sort things out."

Bruce looked into his lap for the right words. "I'm sorry, I don't know what I was thinking."

"It's okay," Krystal said. "I'm glad you didn't come because I realized that I don't want to marry you."

"What?" Bruce asked.

This was better than Eli had hoped for: The kid was getting out guilt free. Now if only Eli could buy Krystal enough drinks to pickle his bastard.

"My mom's put a lot of pressure on me to marry you so the baby would be raised with a mother and father and all that. I finally stood up to her."

"What did she say?" Bruce asked.

"She's probably still crying. And giving my dad hell."

"Whatever you want, I'll do it," Bruce said. "I want to help out with the baby as much as I can."

"That's another thing," Krystal said. "You might not even be the father."

Eli imagined himself at the poker table, drawing dead. His forefinger and thumb made circles around his mouth, flattening the wiry hairs. One of his tells. Bruce was too stunned to speak.

"There was another guy, right around the time it happened. We'd been fighting, and I thought it was over."

"I don't believe this," Bruce said.

Eli wouldn't let Krystal be the one to expose him; if it was coming out, he wanted to be the one in control and see that everything was set straight, right away.

"I slept with her," he said. "I could be—I'm *definitely*—the one."

"That's why I came here," Krystal said to Eli, "to find you and tell you I wanted to know for sure."

Bruce was shrunken and exhausted by the embarrassments that were piling one upon another.

Eli said to him: "She didn't say she had a boyfriend."

"I thought it was over."

To Krystal, Eli said: "And why didn't you tell me to put on a condom? I thought you were on the pill."

"I don't know. I was mad at Bruce." Krystal yelled her next words: "I didn't *mean* to get like this!"

"Then go fix it!"

Krystal's wry expression had thickened into a pained look, her eyebrows pursed and flickering, little flames.

"I want to be certain," she said. "I want both of you to take a paternity test."

"Fine," Eli said.

T.S., whom everyone had forgotten, said Bruce looked like he needed to lie down, and that he'd take him home. Krystal stood and let Bruce out of the booth, kissing him on the cheek as T.S. took him by the arm and guided him away. Krystal sat back down.

"If you won't get an abortion, will you let it get adopted?" Eli asked.

"I don't know that I'd be able to give it up once I saw it."

"Why the fuck are you ruining your life with this?"

Krystal shook her head as if it were too much for him to comprehend. "Don't worry," she said. "I'm not asking you for anything."

"Except money, right?"

"Don't you think you should have to pay for some things?"

No, goddamnit, the answer was no. He could see footing the bill for an abortion.

"Doesn't matter what I think. The law's on your side."

Eli didn't bother showing up at the garage on Monday. Neither, it seemed, did Bruce. While Eli was sitting in the waiting room of the laboratory Krystal had sent them to, Bruce walked in. He smiled at Eli like he was a friend he'd lucked into. Was he smiling because he knew once the results came back, he'd be off the hook, back to a life of comic books and junk food? He signed in and sat next to Eli. Eli asked how he was doing.

"Okay, now that I've had time to think about all this. Will you help Krystal if the baby's yours?"

"I'll have to give her money. But if you're asking if I'll do all that daddy shit, no. It's not for me. And trust me, it's mine."

"If that's true—if it is yours—then I'll feel like I've lost something. Like something's been taken away from me, or a big joke has been played on me."

Eli's name was called.

"Don't feel that way, kid," he told Bruce as he pushed himself out of his seat. "Feel lucky."

Inside an exam room, a young woman took his thumbprint and his picture. From the nametag pinned to her lab coat, he got that her first name was Rupinder. She had this smart hairstyle that ended in little spikes around her neck, and long lashes that drew his attention to her dark irises. It hit him hard that he'd never be with a woman like her, a doctor or whatever she was, he would only ever know women who hung out in bars and would go home with someone like him, someone who lived paycheck to paycheck and didn't saddle themselves with mortgages or families. Only now he was going to be saddled with a kid. Even if he only paid child support and didn't have anything to do with the kid, it would still be out there. It would be his trouble till the day he died. And this doctor or whatever knew it. He imagined her walking into Krystal's school one day to get her smart haircut and feeling sorry for Krystal, who's gotten fat with his bastard and doesn't have a ring.

Rupinder asked Eli to open wide for the swab.

"Wait," he said, holding up his hand. "What if I don't want to do this?"

"I don't understand," she said.

"You know what the deal is, don't you?"

"No. I assure you I only know I'm supposed to collect your DNA."

"This girl thinks I knocked her up, right, and wants me to prove it so she can get her hooks into my bank account."

Rupinder smiled, finding him cute, probably: the big man in tattoos reduced to a frightened child. Bitch.

"So what if I don't let you swab me?"

"If you don't let me swab you, then this girl can ask your father for DNA. Would your father let me swab him?"

"I don't know. I'd rather no one ask him."

"Do you have any brothers?"

Eli's only sibling was a half-sister from his father's first marriage who lived in New York and whom he saw only on holidays. Then the image of some unknown woman's heels digging into Eli's father's wide ass in a far-off hotel room flashed before Eli.

"Not that I know of. Let's just get it over with."

When the swabbing was finished, Rupinder placed the swab in an envelope printed with Eli's personal information. That was how she saw Eli: as small and empty as those few letters and numbers.

"Don't worry so much," she said, sealing the envelope. "It won't be the end of your life if you're the father of this woman's child. It could be a challenge, but where would we be if we were never challenged?"

"What is that? Some mystic bullshit that's supposed to cheer me up?"

"I beg your pardon?"

"I'm sorry. I'm not myself today."

Rupinder, her face gone hard from her long lashes to her buttony chin, shoved the envelope in front of him to be signed across the label. He couldn't recall anything in his life that was so painful to put his name to. He handed the envelope back.

"So, what is it you do for a living?" Rupinder asked.

"I'm kind of in a period of transition."

"I hear the airport is hiring. I'll bet they could use a bigot like you to keep us safe."

After Eli left the laboratory, things again fell like dominos, like that white envelope with all his information printed on it collapsing on itself over and over. He called Laurie to tell her where he'd just come from (there was no sense in waiting for the results, he knew what they were going to say), and she'd cried, and they'd decided to take a break. He called Dave to say he was sorry about everything, and that he'd understand if he didn't want him showing up for work anymore. Dave said he was all wrong—he wanted him to come back; Eli guessed that Dave might've liked the idea of his daughter marrying him. But Eli said he wasn't up for it. He'd pick up his drums that evening. He didn't call his parents. He waited three days for the results to come. The letter informed him he had a 99.99999 percent chance of being the father of Krystal's child.

The letter fluttered on the seat beside Eli, threatening to fly out his pickup's windows, as he sped down 65 toward Shelbyville to have dinner with his parents. Eli's father had just returned from several days away, and as usual, his mother had fussed over dinner: candles on the table, crescent rolls wrapped in a cloth napkin inside a wicker basket, butter on a dish rather than the plastic tray it sat on in the fridge, a bottle of rose wine. She'd even put on a blouse and a skirt and freshened her makeup since getting in from work. She'd huffed at Eli's faded black pearl-button shirt. Eli's father, for all the ceremony surrounding his return, tested his bulk in an American Airlines polo shirt and jeans. With each return home, he seemed to have grown in layers, not only in his barrel-shaped middle, but on his cheeks and arms and even his fingers. He was quiet as they ate, as if he could tell from Eli's jaw, which hadn't unclenched since Friday night, that something was bothering his son. He made only little grunts of agreement or surprise at his wife's updates. After dinner, Eli's mother served them leftover Derby pie, a wide slice for Eli, and a thinner slice for his father. For all the pie's sweetness, Eli couldn't finish his. When his mother had gone into the kitchen to clean up, his father reached his thick arm across the table and stuck the rest of Eli's pie with his fork. "Don't tell your mother," he said.

Eli's father asked him to step onto the back porch with him while he smoked his pipe. In the twilight, the men watched the surface of the pond that the Katz's and their neighbors' houses backed up to. Fish surfaced with a plop, sending expanding rings across the water. The pipe smelled sweetly.

Eli pulled the envelope from his back pocket and handed it to his father.

"What's this?"

"The results of a paternity test. I got someone pregnant. I'm sorry."

"Oh, boy. Don't be sorry," his father said, unfolding the letter. "These things happen. That's how I ended up in my first marriage."

Eli hadn't known this. His half-sister, working for some designer, probably rich and glamorously single, was the accident. He, floundering and having seeded his own bastard, was the one who'd been nurtured when he was only a thought.

"Do you like this girl?" his father asked.

"I barely know her. It was just one of those things."

"What's she want to do?"

"Have it. Raise it by herself, I guess. If I say I don't want anything to do with it, am I being a total shit or what?"

His father sucked on his pipe, thinking.

"Look, if this girl's not putting pressure on you to play house, then don't knock yourself out over it. You don't have to decide right now what you're going to do. Wait and see. You might find that the two of you want to raise the kid."

"I doubt it."

"Or you might find that you only want to do what you're obligated to. But it's not the end of your life. Don't take this the wrong way, but kids aren't all that different from other people—you grow apart from them. You don't stop loving them, but they don't take up as much room in your life. Like your sister, I barely ever talk to her. And when she visits, your mother expects it to be this tearful reunion, but it's not. It's just nice. I'm not sentimental. You slough people off in a way—at least you try to. If you wanted to move far away, I'd say go for it. I wouldn't want to keep you here for my sake. So just wait and find out what your relationship with this kid's going to be. And do me a favor—don't tell your mother till I leave next week."

In his new job as a Transportation Security Officer at Louisville International Airport, Eli had very little time to think about his child growing inside Krystal. He jogged each morning to unlock the energy needed to be on his feet all day, showered, shaved, dressed in his white short-sleeved shirt with TSA on the epaulets, black-and-yellow-striped tie, and black pants, and reported for the afternoon shift. His father had helped him get the job, which so far had him patting down flyers and throwing out tubes of toothpaste and yogurt cups.

That was how Eli began the long wait to find out how much room his child would take up in his life: working flyers through the checkpoints, guessing at their destinations. The bleary-eyed ponchoed kids to Amsterdam, the smart professionals pulling their suitcases on wheels to New York. Thousands every day, their itinerary set solidly in print and clutched in their hands, while he had only the letter from the lab that didn't begin to tell him what to do. Occasionally, he'd find himself laughing at something one of the other TSOs said on break, and suddenly feel generous, and wonder not about the role of the child in his life, but about his role in the child's life. Then he'd return to the checkpoints and let the feeling rise away on the voices that filled the terminal and wait for its return. And wait.

PROCESSION

You are marrying the wrong man.

This is what you're thinking as your father walks you down the aisle. The beaming faces of your family and friends. The string quartet filling the church with Bach. And you're thinking you've picked the wrong guy, what with the shortened lives of his father and uncle and grandfather—all dead from heart attacks. He doesn't smoke and eats right and runs mini-marathons, but still, you're sure he's going to drop dead before he gets his AARP card. You may get a warning shot from his older brother, the canary in the coalmine, but what good will that do?

Or have you got it backwards? As you get closer to the man whose heart (defective as it likely is) has captured your own, you think that he's marrying the wrong woman. Behind the pink ribbons stitched on so many of your t-shirts and windbreakers and fleeces, have the cells already begun to mutate? You've shown him the photo albums of your mother, he knows about your aunt and your grandmother, but still he's waiting for you at the altar with a stupid grin on his face, the short-sighted fool.

You're at the altar now, Father is saying something to your broken families, and your face turns into one of those bittersweet closed-mouth smiles—the kind where your cheeks go up, but the corners of your mouth turn down, the smile you made a lot when your cat was dying. The man you're going to marry (who's allergic to cats) has caught you in this smile, and you know by the way his brows have shot up that he's worried about what you're thinking. So, you give him your biggest, most joyful, freshly-whitened-teeth smile.

And it changes something in you: You warm to the thought of fighting entropy with this man, of creating and preserving beauty and order for as long as it holds out and then letting go with your cheeks up and the corners of your mouth turned down. (You're a physicist—you know about entropy, that it all *dies*. Cats. Husbands. The will to finish your dissertation.) Isn't your wedding a microcosm of that? The lilies look heavenly in the church's natural light, but they'll begin wilting soon. The spread at the reception, the cake, all of it so lovely, will be picked over. The dance floor will expand, then shrink. The party will end.

And then the fight will continue: You will fill your lives to brimming. Fellowships and post docs. The tenure track. A home in a quiet neighborhood with a big garden to tend each year. Children. Maybe you'll get a dog!

Maybe what Father's saying means all this; you haven't been paying attention. As the white gold band is placed on your finger, you're imagining yourself and your husband hiking some hilly trail somewhere, speckled sunlight on your faces, your dog running along ahead of you. You'll do this a lot. It'll be good for his heart.

MAC, BETH

They were sitting on the back deck in the dying light, Mac drinking Scotch, Beth reading the paper. They'd been there for hours, silently, having forgotten (?) to eat dinner, since Mac had come home from work and found Beth in their bedroom, furiously scrubbing the mattress, crying "Out, damned spot! Out!" Mac went to stop her—it was a futile task; the mattress would have to go—and she broke down in violent sobs. He led her to the bathroom to wash her hands, and she scrubbed them raw and red. On the deck, she continued to rub them, occasionally bringing them to her face to smell.

Mac could only guess at Beth's torments. Was it guilt that had stolen her sleep? She'd done nothing wrong, but it would be an obvious, lazy thing for him to say. Fear had taken his own sleep. Fear that they'd squandered their chance.

A mile down the road, the Bankses had just had a healthy baby boy.

How long would they nurse their secret fears? Tomorrow and tomorrow and tomorrow? Every day till the brief candles of their lives were extinguished, would they be walking shadows of themselves?

"Listen," Beth said in a register he'd not heard since before. She didn't want him to listen to her but was drawing his attention to something.

Mac set down his drink and sat up straight, though he was unsure for what he was listening.

"Someone's out there," Beth said.

Out there were the woods that stretched behind their road, hilly and dense with Black Walnut and Oak. They often saw deer there, but now there was a different gait in the darkness. Mac heard it and saw movement, too. He went to the railing for a closer look.

There were men in camouflage trespassing in their woods—what were they doing? Hunting?—and Mac was going to give them a piece of his mind. His other private torment was his rage; after the initial grief came bouts of fear that they would never have a child and a growing rage with no object. Now here was one.

"Stay here," he said.

He went down the deck stairs and charged into the woods, slowed only by his Oxfords' poor grip on the rocky and root-covered ground and the constant snagging of his pants in the underbrush. He lost sight of them—he could barely see anything, it was so dark in there—so he followed their sounds: the crunching of boots, whispered laughter. Sinister, it sounded. As he got closer, the tone of the men's muted words sobered. He'd been heard, though not yet seen, and the risk in this occurred to him, but failed to stop him.

Mac found himself on the barrel end of a half dozen rifles.

"You trying to get yourself killed?" one of the men said. The rifles were lowered, but still threateningly wielded.

"Get out of here," Mac said, hands on his hips to show his resolve. "Go back wherever you came from. You've no right to be here."

"Calm down, fella. We're just passing through."

"No, you're not. Turn around."

"Who died and made you king?"

Mac thrust a pointed forefinger in the speaker's bearded face, and the men shifted back on their heels.

"Has he got a knife?"

"You bring a knife to a gunfight, man?"

"It's not a knife, just a lot of bluster."

It was only a dagger of the mind, but the men saw that Mac was unyielding. The man on the end of Mac's finger turned to the others. "Come on—let's go around this idiot." The men stomped off in the opposite direction of the house.

Mac waited until he could no longer hear their steps, then fumbled through the dark toward the deck light, which Beth had turned on. He emerged from the woods, and Beth met him at the top of the stairs, wrapped now in a shawl. He put his arms around her, massaged her spine.

"Are you okay?" she asked.

"Yeah." There was no sense in frightening her with the details. "You all right?"

"I don't know. I just feel so… vulnerable right now. What's next?"

"I know. I know. But it was nothing. Just a lot of sound and fury."

Mac led Beth to his chair, where he stretched out so she could lie against him. They grew drowsy from their heat. And there they found sleep.

DOLLY DAGGER

"You did a fantastic job, Oscar. You can't put a price on what you've done for me—though I know you will!"

Oscar's client was jubilant, as he ought to have been; Oscar had achieved nearly all of his objectives—more time with his boys being number one. Oscar smiled. It was always better when clients could laugh about his fees.

His client cocked his head to both sides, as if checking the corners to be sure they were alone, and was met only with casebooks. "I'd like to extend an invitation to you," he said. "A little club I belong to."

"What is it, a poker game?"

"More like a fraternity. Guys unwinding. Saturday night, starts up around ten."

Oscar barely remembered his fraternity. A lifetime ago. Law school had crowded out his undergraduate years. Law school's when he lost his hair but gained his shrewdness. Where he met his wife. They passed the bar together. But the marriage buckled under the weight of their careers and the addition of their daughter. All this time later, he couldn't help but admit—if only to himself—that they would've been okay if only they'd gotten through those early years.

Oscar kept up the habits he'd developed as a hungry law student: rise by five, hit the pool, get to work before anyone else. Beat everyone. Weekends, too, he rose at five to swim. He was shit if he didn't get in his laps.

Saturday night, he couldn't sleep. Lily was on his mind. She'd just turned thirteen. He'd taken her to his pool and dinner to celebrate. Even though they were doing laps, she insisted on wearing her new white two-piece. After every lap, she'd come up and have to adjust her top. Afterwards, she emerged from the locker room transformed into her namesake, only inverted: Her curls were damp and well-nourished earth, her green cardigan a delicate stem, her yellow skirt an upside-down flower. At dinner she ordered a tonic with cherries. They shared tiramisu. It was the best date he'd been on in a long time. Maybe what troubled him was that next time he wouldn't be her date.

The cure for sleeplessness was to not try to sleep. Get out of bed. Turn on the television. Drink a glass of milk. Or get out of the house, have a bourbon. Sleep will come out and pick a fight with you. Take your punches and you win. Tonight: Drive to the address his client had given him, have a drink, and sleep would come out of its corner in half an hour.

He put the address in his phone and was certain he'd made a mistake when the map popped up. It was in the old butcher district, where there were now only a few manufacturers surrounded by neighborhoods of shotgun houses. A couple of corner bars. The address was right, though. Maybe the place had been converted into a luxury loft.

His map led him to a brick building with a foyer of frosted glass. He rang the bell, and after a moment his client let him in. Oscar followed him upstairs into a choking cloud of sound—was that Black Sabbath?—and a shrill fog of smoke. It took Oscar back to high school parties. And therein was the appeal: A dozen or more middle-aged men sat upon a patchwork of sofas and chairs around spreads of liquor, cigarettes, and marijuana pipes. There were no wives to judge, no codes to admonish, and no authorities to enforce. A modern speakeasy.

"This place kept me from blowing my brains out during the divorce. Let me introduce you to Snow Bird."

The owner of the debauched loft held court from a leather sectional, surrounded by his subjects. He wore a gray suit and had an aggressive set of lips and a short, wiry beard. The window behind him reflected his figure, so that when he gestured with his hands, he looked like a four-armed beast. On the table in front of him was a rectangular mirror, upon which was the *TIME* magazine logo and the headline: MAN OF THE YEAR. Generous lines of cocaine zigzagged the mirror.

"Please, sit down," Snow Bird said. "You're the divorce lawyer? Too bad I didn't make your acquaintance ten years ago. Or two years ago! What should I call you?"

"Oscar—"

"First names only here." Snow Bird bent over, disappeared a line. "We're like AA that way. We also admit that we are powerless over our addictions. What's your vice, Oscar?"

"I'll take a bourbon, thank you."

Snow Bird pointed toward the kitchen. "Help yourself."

Oscar went to the kitchen and poured a bourbon, straight. He mingled. He enjoyed parties. In law school, he'd not been good at them; he treated his conversation partners like opposing counsel, mounting his evidence, then closing his case. He'd learned, in the parties he'd attended since—rare as they were—to shut up and listen. He'd become curious about people. Enjoyed non-sequiturs. If rhetoric were called for, he was armed with it.

Snow Bird was also making the rounds, and eventually caught up with Oscar and asked him about the Colts' chances this year. While Oscar made his predictions, he caught sight of a girl padding barefoot across the room, as unlikely as a sparrow flitting by. A brown men's sweater (Snow Bird's?) hung loosely on her shoulders, drooped to her bare thighs. She went into the kitchen and emerged a moment later feeding herself apple slices.

"Who's the girl?" Oscar asked.

"I call her Dolly Dagger. Found her squatting downstairs."

Oscar was already disgusted by Snow Bird. He found open self-destructiveness to be the worst kind of vanity. And that this showboat harbored this runaway in his apartment—it was too much! What was going to happen to this little bird among these wolves?

What happened was that the wolves circled her, clapping and shouting. Oscar sensed ritual in this hunt. They started clawing at her. Yelling and pounding on each other. Oscar looked for his client to see whether he would have a partner in freeing her, but his client was working his way inside the circle, bloodthirsty as the worst of them. Then his client reached for her. The girl kind of squawked and dropped her plate, and stainless steel flashed from the oversized sweater, and Oscar's client had a chef's knife at his neck.

"I'll slit his goddamn throat!"

The wolves scattered. Someone turned off the stereo. The room fell quiet except for the panting of each excited creature.

"Dolly!" Snow Bird said. "Put that thing down."

"Don't come any closer."

"You're going to be in a world of trouble if you don't let him go," Snow Bird warned.

"I've *been* in a world of trouble. Killing this animal won't matter."

Oscar's client winced as the knife broke the first layer of skin and blood trickled down his Adam's apple.

"All right, Dolly!" Snow Bird yelled. "That's enough. What do you want?"

"Your keys."

Snow Bird laughed. "And how far do you think you're going to get, little girl?"

"Far enough."

Oscar had been performing mental triage since the appearance of the knife. The first thing this girl needed was to take the knife from his client's throat. Then she needed to get far away from Snow Bird. The last thing she needed was to be found driving a stolen car.

"I'll take you," Oscar said.

The girl looked at him. "I've never seen you here before," she said.

"So maybe you can trust me."

"Go," she said, shoving her captive away.

"I'll take you home," Oscar said.

"That's a laugh. Come on, let's go."

Oscar woke up to a gray dawn at a rest stop somewhere in Illinois. The girl was curled on the backseat of his Legacy, lost in who-knows-what dreams, soon to stir to the hell that was her life. He pitied her to have to be roused into herself each day.

They'd driven west on 74 for a few hours before enough trust (or perhaps it was only exhaustion) had grown between them to hazard stopping for some sleep.

"I'll take you somewhere that can help you," Oscar had said as soon as they were in his car.

"No," the girl said. "No police."

"I'm not talking about the police. A shelter. A place for women and girls."

"I'll tell you where I want to go. Just drive."

Oscar drove. The poor thing was frightened and had little reason to trust him. Better to let her relax for a bit, get her head straight. After a while, he asked how she got mixed up with Snow Bird.

"He had a soft bed, good things to eat. Better things than most guys."

"What about your parents?"

"If I ever see my dad again, I'm going to castrate him."

"Every father's wish."

The girl woke up, stretched, and hugged herself. Oscar eyed her in the rear-view: She wouldn't pass for anything but what she was: someone who'd been discarded too many times. He suggested that she wait in the car while he ran into a department store and bought her something decent to wear, then they'd get her some breakfast. There was a Target a few exits later. The lot was nearly empty this early in the morning, but he parked about three-quarters of the way back.

"You're going to call the police," the girl said.

"No police, I promise."

"I've been made a lot of promises."

"Look—I'll leave the keys in the ignition. If I trust you won't steal my car, you can trust I won't call the police."

Oscar walked briskly toward the open doors. Fifteen minutes later he came back with two plastic bags to find his Legacy still there, his charge in the passenger seat scanning the radio. He took them to a gas station with the restroom doors located on the side of the building so she could change. She came out transformed: The yellow blouse disguised the carved-out places in her shoulders. The jeans fit well and the canvas flats were cute (something he imagined Lily would like).

"You said we could eat now?"

Across the highway, there was a Shoney's bursting with an after-church rush. Oscar ordered coffee for himself and milk for her ("Whole, if you've got it") and two buffets. The girl jostled old biddies for prime scoops of steaming scrambled eggs and greasy hash browns, pecked strips of bacon and sausage links with tongs without regard for the Sunday schoolers whose hands were next in line. "Sweetheart," Oscar said. "Be considerate." When they returned to their booth, the girl slurped her food, taking enormous swallows.

"I think it's best," Oscar said, "that if anyone asks, you're my niece."

The girl took a drink of milk. "Why not your daughter?"

"Fine. Daughter. What's your name?"

She snapped a piece of bacon in her teeth, looked away. "Dolly's fine," she finally said.

The churchgoers left Oscar and Dolly slouching in their booth, bellies sated with fat, mouths rank with coffee and milk, heads doused in sugar. Oscar hoped that in her post-breakfast nirvana, Dolly would accept his offer to take her someplace that could help her, but she refused again. There was something she was hiding, something that gave her pause about accepting any officially sanctioned help.

They drove. Silently for a while. Oscar didn't see her reticence to talk about herself letting up, and though he didn't feel comfortable divulging much about himself, he was glad when she started asking questions.

"This is a nice car," she said. "Snow Bird's place is nice, and he wears fancy clothes, but his car's a piece of shit. I think that other stuff's for show, because I don't think he has that much money. I bet you're rich, though."

Oscar shrugged.

"What do you do?" she asked.

"I'm a lawyer."

"How'd you get to be a lawyer?"

"Very hard work."

"I can work hard."

Oscar smiled.

"You don't think I can work hard? You ever made pizzas before?"

"I delivered them for a few weeks in college, waiting for a summer internship to start."

"Well, taking orders and making them is the *hard* part."

"What happened?"

"The drivers were a bunch of assholes."

The sky had been an unchanging sheet of gray since morning, but now the threat of violence kicked inside of dark, swollen clouds. Rain slapped the windshield. The radio warned them of a storm blowing in from the plains. Lightning and hail. There was nothing to be done until it passed; Oscar could get the lay of the land then, figure out where to take the girl. As it was, someplace to camp until the storm passed was in order. The next exit offered an oasis in a mall.

They sprinted across the parking lot, skipping puddles to save their feet from chill. Inside the foyer, Dolly shook her wings like a soaked bird, hugged herself to warm up. Oscar patted his dome with the sleeve of his blazer. They had trouble getting much beyond the foyer; neither was practiced in walking through malls without purpose like teenagers (even though Dolly surely still was a teenager). It was Oscar who finally nudged them in a direction—right—and got them moving. Each corridor's offerings matched Oscar's expectations without surprise. Stores invited you inside to try on the identities displayed in their windows, identities so incompatible it seemed the stores would be driven apart like repelling magnets. Yet there they lined up, one after another: college sweatshirts here, a new toe sneaker for runners there, lingerie this way. Oscar glanced at Dolly to see if any of these possible lives spoke to her. But the girl's face remained unexcited at each new storefront.

The oversized faces that beckoned from the windows and the all-too-real faces that passed him in little clusters, the songs that wormed into his head two and three at a time from different stores, lighting and snuffing associations faster than he could grab hold of them—after a while it made Oscar lightheaded. But he knew that in a central location would be the food court, where he could get a shot of sugar to his brain to keep him straight.

They ate cheesesteaks and fries and drank enormous Cokes. The heavy patter of rain on the food court's glass roof drowned out the mall's soundtrack, left no openings in which to start a conversation. They sat for a long time. Dolly ate every last shriveled scrap of fry. Oscar checked his watch; it was getting late in the afternoon, and the hard rain wasn't letting up. He realized if he was going to get this girl anywhere today, he would have to do it right now, but what he wanted more than anything was to brush his teeth. All day he'd wavered between ridding himself of her with a quick call to the police ("She's a runaway—found her sleeping in my car") and letting her choose her own fate. Lulled by lunch and the storm, his rational side didn't stand a chance. He hadn't gotten in his laps.

"I saw a hotel as we were pulling in," he said. "I say we head over there. Tomorrow you should go to a shelter or something. I'm going home."

"I don't need a shelter. I've got money," Dolly said.

"Putting it down on a condo?"

"Funny. I can get a place. And a job. Do you think I can find a job here?"

"I don't even know where *here* is! Let's get you some help from social services."

"No, nothing like that."

"Why are you so goddamn stubborn?"

Dolly walked away, done with the conversation. Oscar caught up to her, as she was dashing into the first store she'd shown any interest in: Gymboree. She picked up a tiny cardigan with a brown bird stitched on the bottom.

"Isn't this adorable!" she squealed.

"Sure. Come on, let's get going."

"I want to look some more."

"We have things to get."

"What things?" she petted more outfits as gently as if they were newborns.

"Toothbrushes. And I'm going to get some swimming gear for the hotel pool. I was going to do some laps, that's all."

"Okay," she shrugged. "I don't care."

They left Gymboree and headed to a department store. Dolly's arms were crossed like a child who didn't get a toy she wanted.

"If you want…" Oscar started, "if you want to get in the pool, you can. It won't bother me."

"I might. I'll need a bathing suit."

"If you want to pick out a bathing suit, go ahead. I don't care."

They split up, Oscar trusting that the girl would meet him at the agreed-upon spot in twenty minutes. He was done in ten. She came a few minutes later with two hangers holding what looked like white ribbons. Oscar handed her his MasterCard. The scanner made its electric pop twice before he thought better of having the bikini show up on his statement.

They were registered as Oscar and Lily, father and daughter. First thing after checking in, Oscar went into their bathroom and brushed his teeth, then changed into his swim shorts. He found Dolly lying in the dark on the bed by the windows, facing the closed curtains, her flats kicked off.

He was half-a-day off schedule, in new goggles and an unfamiliar pool, but the discord this created slicked off him in the first turn. He was used to starting each day in a pool; swimming was a prerequisite for treading on earth the rest of the day. He'd begun at his parent's country club, been a middling swimmer on teams in high school and college, kept up a regimen. Lily was a fish by two.

Oscar aimed to get in his usual number of laps. He was interrupted when, in his periphery, Dolly opened the glass door to the pool area. She was laughing. It was the first time Oscar had seen her smile, and he couldn't help smiling back.

"What's so funny?" he asked.

"Your goggles. You look like a dork."

"Just for that, you can't borrow them."

Dolly took off her blouse, which she'd used as a pool cover up, and stepped into the shallow end. She leaned against a side, threw her arms out and let her head flop back, eyes closed. "Thanks for the swimsuit."

"It's fine. You look nice in it."

Oscar regretted it before it was all the way out. But she opened her eyes and lifted her head and said, "I do! Don't ever tell anyone, but when I put it on, I just stared in the mirror for the longest time."

"I won't tell."

There was a pause in which Oscar wanted to return to his laps, but his concentration was broken, so he just waded, watching Dolly and not watching her at the same time.

"You're like a real swimmer," she said.

"Do you like swimming?" he asked.

"No. I mean, I don't really know how to swim."

"How could you not know how to swim? Didn't your parents teach you?"

Dolly dunked her head underwater, came up and slicked back her hair.

"You show me," she said.

"What?"

"Teach me to swim. Come on."

Oscar instructed her for a few minutes by demonstration. Then, inevitably, she kicked off the bottom and her belly landed in his awaiting palms. This was the first time he had touched her, and his hands tingled under her taut skin, careful not to slip too close to the dangerous border regions of breasts and pubic bone. He instructed her until she asked him to take his hands away. She paddled toward the deep end. Her legs kicked but didn't stay up for long. She was swallowed to her chin before she could push off the bottom with her toes. At its deepest, the pool wasn't more than six feet, though the girl couldn't have been more than five-three. She coughed roughly.

"Are you okay?"

She bounced back toward him, arms cutting away from her sides.

"I'm fine. I can do this."

"Don't expect any calls from the Olympic team."

"I just need to work at it."

"Yeah, well don't work at it alone."

The morning was a cloudless sheet of blue. Oscar's mind had cleared, too: Today, he would be done with the girl. He would drop her at a shelter for victims of domestic violence, drive home, and never speak of her to anyone.

Or so he wished. When he returned with a cup of coffee and a newspaper from a nearby gas station, Dolly was hugging the toilet, wiping her mouth with the collar of the IU t-shirt he'd given her to sleep in.

"What's gotten into you?" Oscar asked.

Dolly erupted. Food poisoning? They'd shared a pizza last night, but he hadn't felt a thing. Drugs? Who knows what's been in this poor kid's body? Though he'd been with her for almost thirty-six hours. She laid her head on her arm and closed her eyes. Oscar left her in this respite from her agony. He sat on his bed with his coffee and newspaper, waiting for the pool to open. Despite the caffeine, he dozed off to wake a short time later and find Dolly returned to her bed, sleeping soundly.

Oscar did laps around a couple of rowdy children whose parents were nowhere in sight. Back in the room, Dolly was sitting up, hugging her legs and scanning TV channels. Oscar returned to the gas station to get her a sandwich and some ginger ale. He felt like calling Lily, though he was afraid of her asking about his weekend; he'd never been good at lying to his daughter.

"I'm going for a walk," he said. "I'll bring some more ginger ale when I get back. Then we should check out."

Lily's voicemail answered. Oscar didn't leave a message; he'd simply wanted to hear her light, untroubled voice.

The girl seemed better. After checking out, he'd take her to a shelter. Tell her that's what was happening, whether she liked it or not. In the light of day—literally, the first sunshine he'd seen since getting involved with the girl—he saw what a mess he'd gotten himself into. There was no explaining it, his shepherding the girl—he didn't even know her name!—until she went willingly for help. Were anyone to look at it from the outside, he was just another in the long line of men who had failed this girl.

There was nowhere for him to go except for the mall. He did brisk loops, weaving around the mall walkers, paying no mind to the stores. It wasn't until his fifth time around that he noticed the Gymboree and remembered Dolly's excitement there last night.

Oscar stopped at the store's threshold. There was the cardigan, the little brown bird. Oh god. He had to get back to her.

If only he could swim his way back! The monstrous slapping of feet against ground was for the clods he suffered in every corridor. It would take a lifetime to get back! But he was landbound from here to the hotel, where he hoped to find the girl safely nested in their room.

His hopes were turned to doubts when he pulled into the hotel parking lot. There were the flashing lights of police and fire and ambulance, guests clustered around questions and speculations. The signs of trouble directed him toward the pool. He ran, wearing the mask of someone attached to the source of the trouble, a look that allowed him closer than anyone else to the officials assembled right outside the pool door.

He was asked his name. He was asked if Lily was his daughter. The question confused him; of what concern was Lily?

"I'm sorry, sir, but there appears to have been an accident."

"She's not my daughter," Oscar said.

"I'm sorry, sir?"

"Is she okay?"

"Did you say the young woman isn't your daughter?"

"No."

"Were you staying here with a young woman?"

"Is she okay?"

"I'm sorry, sir. Sir, could you please come with me?"

Oscar tumbled on his legs, his strong legs with which he wanted to push himself off the concrete and into the pool and propel himself toward the sinking girl, arms outstretched. How would he ever answer for not lifting them up?

MY HOLLYWOOD STORY

I was in Clark County Correctional for armed robbery, and I was mixed up in armed robbery because I ran with the wrong types, and I ran with the wrong types because I was caught picking the pocket of someone who organized low-lifes like me into a profitable crime ring. I don't remember why I started picking pockets. But it was the easiest money on the Strip. The house was always supposed to win, but if you rolled out of the Golden Nugget with a winning look on your face, I would gladly put you back in the red. Anyway, I was part of his crew for nearly twenty years. It was not glamorous. I don't doubt that busboys and garbage men earn more and enjoy a better life than I ever did. You don't rest long enough to figure this out until you're locked up.

I escaped from Clark County Correctional because I was afraid it would be too late for me once I served my sentence. Too late for what? I'm not sure. But there was a situation, and an opportunity, and I was out under cover of darkness. I lifted clothes from a truck stop. Did a dine-and-dash at a twenty-four-hour diner. Before I dashed, the waitress said I was a dead ringer for the actor Charlie Grand. "Sorry," I said. "Don't watch much TV."

But the truth was I knew, like the rest of America, about the melting-down TV star. Just didn't feel like conversation. What I couldn't have guessed then was that, briefly but very publicly, I would become Charlie Grand. But first I had to become Randall Blanton.

One of the old crew dealt in stolen identities and threw me Mr. Blanton for free. With this second-rate but criminally clean identity, I went to L.A. and found work with a driving service. It was a black suit and hat, black sedans and limos. I must've developed a reputation among clients as an efficient and quiet driver—I was in hiding, after all—because I was hired out to bigger and bigger clients. I mean movie stars. The rest of my time I spent walking the streets or in a bar somewhere, just to be near regular people. I've always been terribly shy, especially with women. Usually, I ended up sitting somewhere in front of a TV and looking for my clients until I couldn't keep my eyes open any longer. Only then would I go back to my room.

Once, a woman approached me and said I looked like Charlie Grand. She was built like a plank, but nice-looking in a way. Pretty brown eyes. I said my name was Randall. She asked if I got that a lot, and I said sometimes. She asked me other things, but she kept leaning over to hear me answer, like I didn't speak loud enough, and I felt embarrassed by that so I shut down. It was pathetic. Later, in my room, I imagined the conversation happening all over again, making up both sides. I said I was Grand's body double, but only for nude scenes. Big laugh! No, but I'm a driver for a lot of stars. That's fascinating!

I suppose it was only a matter of time before Charlie Grand ended up in the back of my limo. The entertainment news shows had reported that at the height of his meltdown he'd fired nearly everyone around him. The publicists who tried to spin his outbursts as "bad reactions" to prescription drugs, the lawyers who'd settled to the tune of millions with the producers of the hit TV show he'd been fired from—all gone. I figured his firing spree extended all the way down to his driver. So here he was in my limo at two in the afternoon, dressed in a black t-shirt and dark jeans.

He stared in the rearview, asked me to turn around and face him at the next light. "Take off your sunglasses," he says. "The hat, too."

I did as he asked.

He leaned forward to get a look at me. "It's like looking in a mirror. People ever say you look like me?"

"Sometimes, Mr. Grand."

"It's uncanny," he says. "Are you an actor?"

"No, sir, Mr. Grand. Just a driver."

The light changed, and I started driving, and Charlie Grand relaxed into his seat.

"What's your name?" he asks.

"Randall Blanton."

"Randall Blanton? What kind of sorry name is that? I feel sick just saying it. How about I call you Randy?"

"That's fine, sir."

"What's your story, Randy?"

I told him I came from Reno; that's where the real Randall Blanton lived. He asked if I was married, and I said no.

"I'm shopping for new handlers," he says. "New manager, all that. You interested?"

"Interested in what, sir?"

"Working for me."

"Are you offering me a job, sir?"

"You seem like a good guy. Thick skin. You didn't even flinch when I gave you shit about your name. Plus, it could be fun to weird people out with a doppelganger. I could put you in a dress and take myself to the Emmys!" He burst out laughing at this. "No, even I'm not that weird. Think about it, and I'll have my assistant, Nadine, call you. Don't try anything with her. She's an angel, but don't ever tell her I said that."

The next day, I had a message at the driving service to call Nadine. She asked me to come to Mr. Grand's office. The office had a temporary look to it. The waiting room was spare, a leather sofa and a couple chairs, nothing on the walls. There was no reception desk. A young woman's voice called out from an inner office. Nadine's desk had nothing on it but her laptop and iPhone. She looked to be late twenties or early thirties, movie-star attractive. But they all can't make it, I supposed. She was surprised at how much I looked like her employer. He wasn't kidding, she said. After a few questions, she offered me a job as Charlie Grand's personal driver, pending a background check. I accepted. I knew that, given Charlie Grand's instability, this job was less secure, but the salary was considerably higher. And I liked Nadine.

I spent the next couple weeks driving Charlie Grand from meeting to meeting with managers and publicists and all manner of Hollywood types. He was often irritable on both sides of these meetings. I got the feeling things weren't going well. It wasn't surprising after the indefensible things he'd done, threatening to kill his girlfriend and then beating up those prostitutes. At the end of a long day of meetings, I returned him to his home.

"Come on up with me, Randy. Help me put this god-damned day behind me."

A few days earlier, I'd had an enlightening conversation with Nadine in the office. As it was, we were Charlie Grand's entire staff. We'd chatted a bit by this time. She'd come to

L.A. to act but got burned out doing commercials and bit parts. So, the other day, just to be friendly, I asked how things were going. She sighed, kind of sank in her chair.

"Mr. Grand can be demanding, I guess." It was a throw-away comment, but Nadine sat up straight.

"I know Charlie has a reputation, but he's a very talented actor. And deep down, he just wants to be taken seriously. We're going to get him back into films."

"Hey, you don't have to sell it to me."

"I'm sorry, Randy. I'm so used to feeding that line to people just to get a meeting." Then she spoke quieter, even though we were the only ones around. "I know Charlie's a woman-hating nut job, but for some reason he's very sweet to me. He's never come on to me, not even made a comment about the way I look." Then, as if it had just occurred to her: "Do you think he hired me because he's not attracted to me?"

"I think that's impossible."

"And this is a *good* job. It's going to help me network my way up. I'd like to be a producer. And Charlie's been nothing but supportive. I bet he'd help you, too."

"Help me what?"

"Don't you have a screenplay or something? Charlie could help you get it read. You should do whatever he asks. Trust me."

I wasn't a writer, but I still put my trust in Nadine when Charlie Grand asked me to come up. He led me to an enormous living-room area with thick carpeting that whispered under our feet. Installed in the ceiling was a projector aimed at the blank wall that the leather furniture faced. The opulence was immediately clear, but so was a creeping disarray. End tables were littered with prescription bottles and sticky tumblers. The carpet was filthy. No one had cleaned up after Charlie Grand in some time.

He plunged into one of the leather sofas and took out his phone.

"I'm going to get some girls over here, okay?"

"Excuse me, sir?"

"You have a preference? Blondes? Redheads? I want two of the same, so I don't get buyer's remorse."

I must've looked at him like he was speaking Chinese.

"What I mean is, I don't want to see yours and decide I want her instead. Oh, who am I kidding—I'm going to take the hotter one no matter what!"

As he made the call, it became clear to me what he was talking about. When the call was over, he looked at me and said, "Well, we can't have you dressed that way when they get here." He disappeared into another room and returned a minute later with a pair of jeans and a t-shirt. They'd clearly been laundered and folded by someone whose job was to launder and fold a millionaire's clothes. I stepped into a half bath the size of my room and changed into Charlie Grand's threads. I felt like a swaddled baby.

Back in the main room, Charlie had poured us drinks. "Hope you like bourbon. And brunettes!"

I took the bourbon. I was hoping it would settle me. Because here's what I was thinking: There's a woman about to be delivered to me like a present, and I have no idea what to do. A brief rundown of my history with women: When I was a petty criminal, my girlfriends were runaways and strippers (often both) and liked to party, so as long as I had a little money and could keep the good times rolling, they were happy. But as soon as things got tight, they'd bail. There was nothing about *me* that kept a single one of them around. Since I'd become Randall Blanton—Randy to everyone by now—I wanted to fly right and meet a regular woman, someone who'd like me for just being me (setting aside that who I am is a great big lie). Someone like Nadine, not that she'd ever go for me. It had only been a few months, but I was starting to doubt any regular woman would be with me—it was still *me*, after all, running around in Randall Blanton's name. If I wanted female companionship, it was likely going to have to be with L.A.'s bottom-feeders. I was clearly beneath Charlie Grand-grade prostitutes. So why was he sitting across from me looking slightly bored, like we were waiting on pizza?

Charlie pitched his movie idea to pass the time. He was sick of all the trends: movies about fast cars, comic-book superheroes, lovable dogs. He wanted to do something big, something that would indict Wall Street, Washington, and the War on Terror, and play in blue and red states. Something that would bring people together. Something Oscar-worthy. He had no idea what the plot would be but knew that he would be the hero. An American Hero. Probably ex-military, called upon to use his superb physical skills and razor-sharp intellect to save America's fate. The leading lady would have to be someone new. I suggested Nadine, but he didn't hear.

Then the girls arrived. I was immediately of two minds about them: They looked like the sorry girls I'd run around with for twenty years, dressed in halter tops and short skirts and high heels. But they were stunning versions of those girls. All the lines were right, there wasn't anything extra. You couldn't have ordered up a better plaything if you were someone like Charlie Grand.

Charlie set us all up with bourbon. He claimed one of the girls and brought her to the sofa. Mine sat in a chair by the chair I was in. Charlie told them his movie idea.

For a while, he talked and the girls laughed and I sat there. The whole time, he was petting his girl's bare leg and she was touching his hair. When he said I was his bodyguard, my girl got out of her chair and came and sat on my lap. I looked in my girl's green eyes, which were the only thing that let you know there was a person in there, and said, "Excuse me." I set her on the chair's wide arm and got up and started to leave.

I figured that was that. I would go back to just being Charlie Grand's driver (unless he fired me), and pine over Nadine. If no one was going to have me unless Charlie Grand was bankrolling it, I was ready to give up and spend all the energy I'd otherwise waste on women yearning for the best woman I knew, even if she'd never want me back. But Charlie had chased me down in his foyer.

"Where are you going?"

"I don't belong here, Mr. Grand."

"Why are you insisting on acting like you don't deserve what I'm giving you? You might've been a worthless nobody when you were beating around the desert doing whatever you used to do, but now you're one degree away from Hollywood royalty. I'm King Midas, and I touched you, so now you're gold. Start acting like it."

The next morning, a faint knocking woke me. I was in one of Charlie Grand's bedrooms. The knocking was someone at the front door, but I didn't rush to answer it. I figured Charlie would get it. I remembered what had happened was that I'd gone back with Charlie. Him talking to me in the foyer was kind of like when I was caught picking the wrong pocket when I was still a teenager. That man had chosen me to be a petty criminal, which was not so good.

Now Charlie had chosen me to be, I don't know, part of his entourage. Which could be very good. Maybe I would write a screenplay. Anyway, it was a relief to leave things up to fate. I'd come back inside. At some point I fell asleep.

The knocking was unrelenting. I picked up the clothes Charlie had given me and put them on so I could go see who the hell it was. It was Nadine.

"Charlie," she says. "I am so sorry, but I can't get a hold of Randy. I'll take you myself."

"Slow down," I say. "What's going on?"

"I can't find Randy. He was supposed to pick you up this morning. You look awful. Let's go inside and get you freshened up."

She pushed me inside and walked briskly toward Charlie's master bedroom and into his closet, where she grabbed a new outfit.

"Put these on, and do something with your hair."

I stepped into the master bathroom. Charlie was passed out on the floor, naked as the day God made him. I covered his lower half with a towel to give him a shred of dignity.

"Mr. Grand," I whisper, nudging his shoulder.

He gave a little groan; he might've meant to say, "Go away."

"Are you all right?" Nadine asks from the bedroom.

"Just fine," I say. I whisper to Mr. Grand, "You've got to get up. You're supposed to… I'm not sure, but you're supposed to do something."

"Go away," was absolutely clear this time.

So, I dressed and did something about my hair. I figured I owed it to him.

Nadine put me in the back of her car and started giving me the who's who about the people we were having lunch with. Another agency she was trying to match Charlie with. The names left me as soon as I heard them.

Then she says, "I'll interview some new drivers as soon as possible."

"Hold up," I say. "Let's not do anything rash."

The posh restaurant we pulled up to was one I'd taken Charlie to a few times. I had left Charlie at the front door, then parked around back. Once, the breeze had carried this wonderful, heady, oyster smell from the deck. The next few meals I ate, I felt like I was eating from a grease trap. But this time, Nadine and I got out and let the valet park the car. The maître d' greeted us warmly and led us to the deck where, at a table under a trellis (for privacy, I'm now sure), the agency people were waiting. After the introductions, it went about like this: Nadine and the woman from the agency spoke earnestly about Charlie's career, the guy from the agency did a lot of nodding and looking thoughtful, and I put my energy toward savoring every morsel the waitress placed in front of me. Fresh spinach with quail eggs! Slices of honeydew wrapped in prosciutto! When those were all gone, I gave the waitress this timid wave and she rushed over. I asked, "Would it be possible to get another plate of those melon things?" And she was back quick. When the thing seemed to be running down, Nadine looked at me expectantly. Between not paying attention and not understanding what I'd heard, I really had no idea what had been said.

"Well," I say. "This all sounds very good. And I want to be in movies again. So I say we get in bed together!"

The agency people got all excited over this declaration and started making arrangements with Nadine, and I was able to tune out again. I'd come with Nadine as Charlie's employee; "surrogate" wasn't in the job description, but he'd been good to me and I thought he'd appreciate my efforts to cover for him. But things were conspiring to make me feel like I was Charlie Grand: Nadine's attention, the never-ending food and wine, the fawning of the agency people. I felt like a king. When Nadine and I had left the restaurant, I asked her to walk with me for a bit before we got back in the car.

I say, "Let's cancel the rest of my day. Do something fun."

She looked at me like I'd gone crazy. Like Charlie had gone crazy.

"Come on," I say. "We'll get to know each other better."

I think she was about to say yes, and I was going to spend the day with best woman I'd ever known, even if she thought I was Charlie Grand, when I was only Randy Blanton pretending to be Charlie Grand, and really, I was only me pretending to be Randy Blanton. Then the paparazzi showed.

"Mr. Grand! Mr. Grand!" It wasn't a mob or anything, just a couple of jerks, but they made a hell of a noise. It was all, What do you have to say about this or that terrible thing Charlie Grand had allegedly (and probably) done. I think if they'd shown up a moment earlier, I would've said something very different than I did. Something like, I'm Charlie Grand! Hollywood royalty! I don't have to answer to you parasites! Come back when I'm nominated for an Oscar—then maybe we'll talk! But the possibility of having to keep up with Nadine had collapsed my heightened sense of self. I was really just me, which wasn't much. So I said what I would've said if I were Charlie Grand.

"Look, I regret the way I've behaved. There's no question, I've done some terrible things. I apologize to anyone I may have hurt, and hope they'll find it in their hearts to forgive me. I apologize to my fans, too. I'm ready to get my career started again, and I hope you'll support me."

That's about it. Nadine rushed me back to Charlie's. Charlie was sobered up by now. The three of us watched the "Contrite Charlie Grand" clip over and over. It was everywhere. They were astonished, but not angry. It was decided that my deception would be kept a secret for now. Charlie signed with the agency Nadine and I had lunched with.

Now that Charlie's in a hit movie and has the goodwill of his fans, I figure the story can be told. And telling it shows me how far I've come; I think a lot more of myself these days. So thanks for listening. Hope your editor likes it. Randall Blanton's a pseudonym, of course. If you want to get back in touch, here's Nadine's card. She knows how to reach me. Well, I have to run. Got a meeting about my screenplay. Wish me luck!

THE COMMISSION OF INQUIRY

Upon reaching the city that bore his name, Pierre Savorgnan de Brazza became troubled by a suspicion that he would not leave Africa alive. The entire commission was depleted by the last four-and-a-half months; a three-week steamship passage from the port of Marseille to Libreville, nearly three more weeks sailing down the coast to the mouth of the Congo, a sluggish train ride to the interior, and rough journeys by steamer to the isolated forest outposts of French Equatorial Africa. The days were either rainy or hot, and a steam hung about at all times, sapping the commission's strength. The mosquitos were unrelenting. And the colonial administrators from whom the commission was seeking answers were impossible to crack—until the discovery of the concentration camps. With the revelation of the atrocities, Pierre was bearing a shock to his psyche that was not shared by any of the other commissioners, not even Thérèse. He was certain he'd contracted dysentery, too.

When Thérèse awoke on the morning of the trial, she found her husband sitting upon the bed, troubled. His face was largely unchanged by the deprivations they'd lately suffered; the strong T formed by his nose and brow and his high cheeks and short beard made him as handsome as ever. But his startling blue eyes seemed dimmer.

"What's the matter, Pierre?"

"I awoke with the feeling… that I may never leave Africa."

"Don't talk that way! Don't frighten me with unfounded *feelings*."

"If I don't—"

"Stop!"

"Listen. If I don't, you must ensure that my desk-trunk is returned to Paris. My notes are in a secret compartment inside."

"A secret compartment?"

"I was afraid that I would have to implicate many administrators. A prediction that has been borne out. I couldn't risk my notes being destroyed by one of these criminals."

"A secret compartment, then."

"Summon Georges Vuitton to the ministry to open it for M. Clèmentel."

"*You* will deliver your report."

"Promise me you'll do this."

"It's unnecessary, but I promise."

Pierre got up from the bed and went to the toilet, cramping. When he finally dragged himself back, Thérèse suggested that he eat something. Pierre wanted only coffee.

"I know you're tired."

"I'm drained, dear."

"Your strength will return. It always does. I won't allow you to die here. If you do, Clèmentel will bury your report and parade your corpse throughout the Republic, crying, 'Look upon the martyr of the French Congo!' all to glorify himself."

The commission of inquiry had been formed in response to the Toquè and Gaud scandal, which had broken in *Le Matin* in February. "The Black Man's Executioners" excited the public with a tale of incredible cruelty: Fort Crampel's top administrator, Georges Toquè, and a subordinate,

Fernand Gaud, had been charged with the murder of Papka, a young Congolese man. It was Bastille Day of the prior year, and Toquè and Gaud wanted to enliven the holiday for the other handful of Frenchmen at the outpost. Toquè suggested the execution of Papka, whom they had arrested for murder. Papka had been bound by rope and thrown into a narrow hole. Gaud pulled Papka from the ground and grabbed a stick of dynamite. He then forced the dynamite into Papka's anus, lit the fuse, and ran for cover. "The prisoner screamed. An explosion rang out. Bloody debris was projected a great distance."

The Minister of Colonies, Etienne Clèmentel, quickly announced that a commission of inquiry would be formed to investigate the charges against Toquè and Gaud. Etienne was sickened by the tale. There were likely details that *Le Matin* had gotten wrong, but he had no doubt that something monstrous had happened at Fort Crampel, and whoever was responsible needed to be brought to justice. The presence of a commission of inquiry at the trial would increase the likelihood of that outcome. But it was critical that the commission find no more Toquès or Gauds. Abuses that would rouse the public against France's presence in Africa needed to be dealt with swiftly and quietly.

Etienne, having announced the commission, considered which colonial inspector to appoint its head. M. Dubard? No—he couldn't put this burden on the old man. Besides, there were many young strivers who would exculpate the ministry—though appointing someone who hadn't yet earned the prime minister's respect would give away the game. But appointing a veteran inspector of whom the prime minister approved carried a different risk—the risk of commissioning a condemnation of the ministry.

Regrettably, Etienne resolved to call upon M. Dubard. There was no one else whom the prime minister respected *and* who would fiercely protect the ministry.

"You want me to investigate… what are they being called? 'The black man's executioners'? I'm sorry, Etienne—I don't believe I'm quite right for this."

"It's very simple: Toquè and Gaud have already been charged and will be tried in Brazzaville. A commission of inquiry needs to be present, that's all."

"That's all? What about an investigation?"

Etienne paused. He owed the old man the truth.

"The Ministry of Colonies *cannot* afford comparisons to Leopold. The world is coming to know of his brutalities. M. Twain's little book is seeing to that. This commission of inquiry's charge is to assure the Republic—and the world—that French Equatorial Africa is mutually benefi-cial to France and Africa. You would be doing your country a great service."

"All the same, I think I'd rather avoid this mess. If the commission finds that these men at Fort Crampel are not aberrations… that, God forbid, our men are chopping off Africans' hands or worse… do you want the commission to lie?"

Something rose in Etienne's throat, and for a moment he could not speak. "The Ministry requires a favorable report."

"So you called me?"

"I meant no disrespect."

"Find someone else. And for your sake, find someone fast—before M. Brazza noses his way into this!"

Pierre did not have to nose his way onto the commission. He received a letter notifying him that Prime Minister Loubet would be announcing to the press his wish to see the former commissaire of the colony, the famed explorer and national hero Pierre Savorgnan de Brazza, come out of retirement and lead the Minister of Colonies' commission of inquiry. Pierre shared the letter with Thérèse, who was in the children's room. She stood up with little Antoine in her arms.

"What is this?"

"A request, as it were, from the Prime Minister."

Thérèse scanned the letter. "You're going back to the Congo?"

"I must. This is a chance to right what has been corrupted in my absence."

"Then I am going with you."

Pierre had first come to the Congo in 1875, and his exploration was slow, methodical, a mystery to his superiors in the French Navy—and often to his own men. He befriended each tribe as he traveled further into the interior along the Ogowe River, a journey that, while laborious, resulted in his winning for Paris the western side of the Congo, rather than letting Henry Morton Stanley take the whole of it for Leopold through brute force. While Stanley dynamited the forest to make his road, Pierre exploded fireworks in celebration of his new friendships to make his. Within five years he had established the French colony. As commissaire in the 1880s and 1890s, Pierre led a colony that was held in great contrast to Leopold's on the other side of the river. Even when the demand for rubber exploded during the bicycle craze and Paris put pressure on the commissaire to increase production, Pierre declined to resort to Leopoldian tactics. There would be no beatings by rhinoceros-hide whips to induce labor nor any of the other tortures that Leopold and his men had invented. Paris was faced with the unenviable choice of firing a national hero or watching the financial collapse of the French Congo.

Pierre was dismissed in 1898.

Etienne was horrified to read the prime minister's announcement. He had no choice but to appoint M. Brazza head of the commission of inquiry. Appointing anyone else would be risking losing his own position and raising the public's suspicion. In the public's mind, there was no one more suited to investigate the colony; Brazza knew the interior and the Congolese better than anyone and could be trusted to uphold what was best for the Republic and for the Congo. But if Brazza produced a report that did not portray Toquè and Gaud as exceptions to the rule of benevolent administration, it would expose French Colonial Africa to comparisons to Leopold's Congo. The press would bury Etienne and his ministry.

Etienne summoned Brazza to his office to discuss the commission of inquiry's charge. When Brazza arrived, he was accompanied by a bespectacled young man with a trim mustache. He was not with the ministry. Brazza introduced him as Fèlicien Challaye. The name was familiar to Etienne, though he wasn't sure why.

"M. Challaye will be my secretary on the commission," Brazza announced. "I fully trust him to report the state of the colony truthfully."

Etienne now placed the name. Challaye was a journalist—of the radical sort. The sort that Etienne did *not* want investigating the colony.

"He's… you're appointing him to the commission, then?"

"I assure you that his work will be to the satisfaction of the ministry."

"Have you been to the Congo, M. Challaye?"

"No."

"Very hot. Rainy season coming up, too. Plagues of mosquitos."

"I'm very well-travelled, but thank you for the warning."

"Pierre, I'll give you some of the best men from the ministry to fill out the commission."

"You needn't go to the trouble. I prefer to choose the men myself."

"Very well."

Etienne had not even broached the subject of the commission's charge and already he felt as if the meeting had escaped his control. He realized he was slouching and worrying his mustache, so he sat up straight and put his hands together in front of him on his desk and started over.

"I asked you here to discuss the commission's objectives. The charges against Toquè and Gaud are very serious, and the ministry must demonstrate to the Republic that such crimes are extremely rare and will not be tolerated."

"My commission will demonstrate to the Republic *whether* such crimes are extremely rare," Brazza said.

"Yes, of course," Etienne assured him. "Should you find other cases of men behaving like those monsters, they of course must go in your report. Should you find any individuals like that, they must be removed from their posts. The ministry won't tolerate any bad actors. Not on my watch. Not in our peaceful, mutually beneficial colonies. I'm sure the presence of men like Toquè and Gaud in the colony you founded aggrieves you greatly. I'm sure they're very rare, but we will root them out."

"From where does your optimism come?" Brazza asked. "Toquè and Gaud instill in me only fear about the state of the colony."

Etienne had no answer for this. "And this is to be done as soon as possible."

"A proper investigation will take time. I'm prepared to stay as long as it requires."

"I can give you six months."

"That's all?"

"The Republic must be assured of order in the colonies. I expect a report by the end of September."

"We will spend half of our time in transit!"

"That gives you three months to investigate."

"One might say the ministry doesn't want an investigation. But that is what the prime minister asked of me. He did not assign me the duty of saving your ministry."

"Gentlemen, please. Our fidelity is to the Republic. Surely, we all agree on that. It's imperative to eliminate threats to its colonies. The commission, by demonstrating the difference between French Equatorial Africa and the Congo Free State, will rid us of the threat that the monsters Toquè and Gaud have raised. Imagine the damage if we're made to look even glancingly like Leopold."

"My fidelity is to the truth," Challaye said.

Pierre smiled, knowing he had chosen his secretary well. Then he said to Etienne, "We will hide nothing. The commission will see that threats are exposed and the colony is returned to its former glory."

After selecting the most trustworthy men to fill out the commission—nine in all, men with experience in Asia and the South Pacific as well as Africa—Pierre called upon the Louis

Vuitton company. For his earlier journeys to Africa, Pierre had relied on M. Vuitton for beautiful camphor-wood trunks that protected his clothing and provisions from the humid climate. They had even kept his fireworks dry. One trunk converted into a bed, making it possible for Pierre to rest in even the most uninhabitable reaches of the forests. Now Pierre needed something special. The company quickly produced a trunk to his specifications. Within the trunk was a desk. When the lid was lifted, a writing surface was revealed; the front panel could be lowered to reveal, below the writing surface, a row of three drawers, and below the drawers were five compartments. In the rear of the center compartment was a false wall, behind which Pierre planned to hide his most damning notes of the colonial administration. His and Fèlicien's meeting with Clèmentel had served to warn him that the commission could not expect cooperation from the administrators; he was certain Clèmentel would instruct his successor, Commissaire Gentil, to obstruct the commission at every turn. (That is in fact what Clèmentel had done following the meeting.) The ministry was clearly hiding something, and Clèmentel's administrators would go to great lengths to keep it hidden—even raiding the trunks of a national hero. Pierre didn't tell anyone, not even Therèse, about the secret compartment.

The commission of inquiry left in April and arrived in the capital in mid-May. The Meridien Hotel gave the commissioners a merciful respite from the constant motion of waterways and railroads. Therèse, Fèlicien, and the nine commissioners from the ministry fell into their beds and relished the solidness beneath them. Therèse did not share her explorer husband's experiences, nor his vigor, but pride kept her from showing her weariness to him. Fèlicien, though he was not built like Pierre—he was short and slightly pudgy—had a constitution for enduring hardship and did not complain. And among the nine commissioners from the ministry, even the most deskbound men shored up their strength for Pierre, whom they all admired. But Pierre could tell they were weary and permitted them a few days of rest. Fèlicien reminded him of the constraint Clèmentel had put on them: "We must be back in the capital by mid-August for the trial. Our investigation will have to be complete by then if we are to deliver it by September's end." But Pierre insisted. "We have a difficult road ahead of us," he said. "So rest while you can." Pierre would not rest, however, and called upon Commissaire Gentil immediately.

Brazzaville had changed little in the seven years since Pierre had been dismissed. There were a few more administrative buildings, the church had added some annexes, and the trading posts now belonged exclusively to French firms. The English firm, Hatton and Cookson, and all the European firms had been forced out when Paris parceled the colony out to French firms, each having a monopoly over their parcel, after the practice of Leopold. Pierre's residence was now the home of Commissaire Gentil.

Pierre sought Gentil at the Government Palace, a two-story structure with a low-pitched roof, the eaves of which extended to a perimeter of columns and arches. Pierre remembered sitting under the eaves and looking out upon the wide dirt road that led to the palace when messengers from the ministry arrived to remove him. He'd gone peacefully. Passersby, French, English, European, and Congolese, praised him and cursed the men who'd been sent to recall him. Not everyone was upset to see him go; newer administrators and French traders who stood to benefit from the monopoly system they saw as Paris' next move in the colony gave cursory nods to their commissaire and knowing looks to each other. Pierre wished Gentil were sitting there now to receive him; the reversal would have delighted him! During the commission's travels, Pierre had grown firm in his mission to stop whatever Gentil was doing to bleed the colony of its resources and return it to a mutually beneficial state. But no one was there, and an administrator informed Pierre that the commissaire was busy with the bishop. Pierre was to wait at the Meridien for the commissaire to send for him. Which might be days, as there was much for the commissaire and the bishop to discuss.

Pierre went straight to the church, where a priest informed him that the bishop and the commissaire were not to be disturbed. "Give the bishop my best, Father," Pierre said before taking his leave. "And pray for the colony."

It pained Pierre more deeply than he had anticipated as he walked up to his former residence. The residence was similar to the palace, only smaller. Pierre sat in a chair on the lower porch and crossed his feet upon a low table, making himself at home, as it were. Gentil could not hide from him here.

The day began to fade. Pierre resisted the urge to return to the hotel and update Thérèse and Fèlicien; he did not want to miss Gentil. As the sun was setting on Pierre's right, three shapes approached the residence from the road. The middle one was quite short compared to the other two. It was revealed to be the commissaire flanked by two administrators.

"M. Brazza!" Gentil bellowed, puffing out his chest. "I hope I've not kept you long from your Congolese friends. I know you're very fond of them."

"I am here on their behalf."

"I know whom you serve."

"I serve the prime minister. Whom do you serve?"

Gentil dismissed his escorts and invited Pierre into the parlor. Gone were Pierre's intricately carved African statues, which had once adorned every end table; in their place were objets d'art of the Republic. A bronze and marble mantel clock sat where Pierre had once hung a mask.

"Toquè and Gaud's trial is not for six weeks. I daresay you don't need that long to investigate them." Gentil's waxed goatee jumped as he spoke. "You may see them right now if you wish."

"The commission was not sent to give legitimacy to the trial; it was sent to investigate the colony's administration."

"*I* am the colony's administration."

"Then I shall start with you." Pierre, having established his commission's agenda, stood and told Gentil that he and his secretary would see him at the Government Palace the following morning.

Commissaire Gentil welcomed Pierre and Fèlicien to his office in the Government Palace. Fèlicien had insisted on joining Pierre, claiming that it was critical for his reporting. The men were waited upon by a young Congolese woman, who served them with a forced smile.

"I'm going to be perfectly clear," Pierre said. "My commission requires the cooperation and forthrightness of every administrator in the colony."

"What would make you expect anything less?" Gentil said, laughing.

"M. Clèmentel. I've no doubt he's charged you with protecting the colony's reputation."

Gentil's smile fell away. "M. Clèmentel expects me to do my job."

"And the Prime Minister expects me to do mine. Which is to investigate the colony with or without your cooperation. A thorough report will be in Clèmentel's hands by the end of September. Whether it satisfies his wishes is not my concern."

"And you've brought a radical to write it?" Gentil said. Fèlicien shot up, but before he could speak, Gentil continued: "Who will believe him? Clèmentel? The prime minister? I doubt it."

"I will vouch for him. Do you doubt they will believe me?"

Fèlicien settled down and, rather than speak up for himself, let Pierre's point sink in.

"M. Brazza, perhaps in your absence you've forgotten the economic disaster that your administration was to the colony. If you had been permitted to stay the course, the French firms would've gone broke, and the Blacks would have taken everything you'd worked so hard for. Turned it all back to barbarity."

"I should like it to be proved that you've not turned it to barbarity," Pierre said.

"What are you talking about?"

"Toquè and Gaud."

Gentil waved a hand dismissively. "Their actions don't represent the colony."

"I should like it to be proved," Pierre insisted.

"Then the colony shall prove it. Go to Fort Lamy. It's a remote outpost up the Ubangi, not as far as Fort Crampel. It should reassure you of the state of the colony. Then come back to the capital, let the commissioners have a holiday. You too, M. Challaye." Gentil gave his head a tilt that Pierre would have read as sympathetic if he didn't suspect other, hidden meanings. "Don't you think you deserve to enjoy the city the Republic honored with your name, M. Brazza? Have a holiday with your wife. Don't traipse around the forest until it kills you."

The commission's respite ended, and they boarded a steamer for the journey up the Ubangi River, a tributary of the Congo and a key trade route. Upon its banks were several of the colony's outposts. The commission would reach Fort Lamy first. Pierre guessed that Gentil had ordered the men there to put on a good show for the commissioners, and should that fail to appease them, frustrate them by refusing to cooperate—whatever it took to keep the commission's investigation from reaching further upriver to Fort Crampel and other outposts.

Pierre had told Therèse that Gentil hoped that the commission would return to the capital after visiting Fort Lamy and idly await the trial. "Which I'm certain he has a tight fist around, too." Therèse assured him that the ministry men would follow him as far upriver as they could reach in the time they had to investigate. "They adore you."

As rain pelted the river, Pierre, Therèse, and Fèlicien sat under the low roof at the rear of the steamer, while the ministry commissioners managed the ship. Their pith helmets shielded their faces and beards, but their wool uniforms were soaked. They smiled wryly to each other about their plight, but never once complained to Brazza. It was an honor to have been chosen for his commission, and they would do anything to see that the investigation was completed to his satisfaction. They dutifully waited upon him and his wife and assisted his secretary. They carried his trunks, and if the need should arise—God forbid it—they would carry him. It was a brotherhood the men would remember fondly for the rest of their lives, in spite of the tragic conclusion of their expedition and the suppression of the commission's report.

Days passed and the rain gave way to steamy heat. There was little for the commission to do as they floated along except play cards and nod to passing traders, hard-faced men in sweat-stained clothes who, once they saw Brazza aboard, looked upon them with disdain. The only Congolese they saw were solitary men who accompanied traders, liaisons to the native population; they would not risk their positions talking to the commission, and none of the commissioners asked them to.

When the commission reached Fort Lamy, they nearly passed it; it was nothing more than a handful of small one-story buildings with thatched roofs. Only the shorter side of the long trading post and a rudimentary dock could be seen from the river, and those were nearly hidden by thick, hanging boughs. The steamer pulled up alongside the dock, and the commission filed out, the ministry men first, followed by Fèlicien, Thèrese, and finally Pierre. A single Frenchman watched from the shore with his arms crossed as the commission emptied out of the boat.

"You've brought the entire ministry, M. Brazza!" he called. "Do you really think this show of force is going to help you gain back your colony?"

"I've not come to gain back the colony for myself," Pierre said.

"Then for whom? The Blacks?"

It would not be placation, then, but obfuscation. Pierre cut through the ministry men and joined Fort Lamy's top administrator on the shore. Thèrese followed. The three of them went to the administrator's office/residence, where Pierre's questions about the treatment of Congolese traders and porters were met with misdirection. The ministry men and Fèlicien began their investigation, though it quickly became clear that there were more of them than there were men in all of Fort Lamy. The men they talked to—five in all—were, unlike their leader, cooperative and friendly. In fact, they seemed to relish the presence of the commissioners. Their answers suggested that nothing like the crimes allegedly committed at Fort Crampel had ever occurred there. The Congolese, if they were to be believed, were treated with respect and paid fairly for their goods and labor.

"Where are the Congolese?" Pierre asked.

"In the forest. Collecting, I hope."

"Are any due at the outpost today?"

"Who can tell? They'll have to lay about their huts a good while first, lazy creatures."

"By what means do you ensure adequate production?"

"There are no means by which you can make them work."

"Exactly what means have you and your men tried?"

The administrator stalled. "We are not dynamiting them, if that's what you're asking. Have you any fireworks? Perhaps a bit of Brazza's magic would help production!"

Fort Lamy's production, however, was not suffering, according to the records the ministry men had uncovered. Congolese men were delivering massive amounts of rubber and ivory to Fort Lamy for substandard prices; French traders were taking those goods downriver to meet steamships bound for Europe.

"How is it that the Congolese collect this much rubber?" asked Fèlicien.

One of the Fort Lamy men replied, "Have you anything to read?"

"I'm sorry?" said Fèlicien.

"Newspapers? Books? Anything at all you can spare? We so rarely receive anything to read."

The commission left Fort Lamy with only circumstantial evidence: records that proved the efficacy of its collection of the forest's natural resources. No explanation for the high production coupled with low prices could be extracted from the men there—no threats, no intimidation, no violence. The commission found more of the same with every outpost they investigated; every leader was brusque with Pierre, and every camp was plagued by ennui. Congolese were scarce. At the third outpost, Thèrese said to Pierre, "I'll bet Gentil scared the Congolese away for your visit."

On the last day of June, over a month since their arrival at Fort Lamy, the commission finally saw a gathering of Congolese. The commission did not expect to find any trace of Toquè and Gaud's crime at Fort Crampel—it was a year since the alleged atrocity had occurred—but its new administrators sought to prove beyond doubt that the Fort Crampel of Toquè and Gaud was an aberration—if not a total lie—by treating the commission to an evening of dances by a group from the nearby village. Papka's village.

After a day of questioning the polite administrators and perusing their records, Pierre, Thèrese, and Fèlicien settled into chairs in the center of the camp, the ministry men standing behind them, to enjoy the performance.

"What do you think is Gentil's game, here?" Pierre asked Fèlicien. Fèlicien didn't answer; he stared at the forest on the other side of the thatched-roof buildings.

"I'm sorry. I can't help imagining that poor man bracing himself for… for the explosion. Do you think this was the spot?"

Before Pierre could reply, the dancers appeared on the dirt plaza before them. In the eyes of every Frenchmen present save Pierre, the dance was a flurry of barbarism: The villagers' movements were rhythmic enough to be called dance, but it was dance of a lower culture. Animalistic. But Pierre, whatever was in his heart regarding the equality of the races, saw grace and beauty. The movement of the dancers' arms evoked Pierre's fireworks. They had dazzled the Congolese! And the drums that accompanied the dancers hit sweet notes of Pierre's past, too: sleeping under the stars in his bed-trunk!

"It's lovely," said Thérèse.

Pierre was pulled out of his reverie by the motion of one of the dancers: He had begun to mime a man in shackles! Pierre read in it the revelation of a concentration camp. He turned around and saw that the commission's hosts were oblivious to the meaning of the dancer's movements. He watched the man's dancing a moment longer, then, assured of the dancer's message, shot up in his chair and yelled for the administrators to take him to the camp immediately. There followed a commotion as the administrators tried to ease him and the dancers fled to their village. "Let them go," Pierre commanded. "Take us to the slave camp, now."

A reluctant administrator led the commission down a forest path to a hidden building, a low thing from which an awful reek emitted. The door was chained shut. "Open it," Pierre demanded. An administrator whose face was drained of color approached the lock and opened it. A ministry man pulled the door back on rusted hinges; the cloud of reek expanded; the ministry men, mouths and noses covered by pith helmets, entered the building, from which emerged cries and whimpers.

A moment later, one of the ministry men carried out an ashen, wasted woman. No one was sure whether she was alive or dead. More ministry men followed with more women and children, too. Pierre joined them and carried out a young woman with a baby crying at her breast. Thèrèse could no longer contain her rage and charged toward the administrators, but Fèlicien contained her. "You monsters!" she cried.

The concentration camp held over a hundred women and children from Papka's village. Fèlicien included the following in his report: "Fort Crampel's administrators, who had earlier denied acts of coercion, admitted upon the discovery of their slave camp that the prisoners had been taken to ensure that the village's men would collect adequate amounts of rubber and ivory. The prisoners were crammed into the camp so tightly that almost all movement was restricted. Their muscles atrophied and their faculties withered. They starved. Fully half of them died, including a woman who gave birth inside the camp. The baby was adopted by a survivor, though its chances for survival are difficult to tell."

"Have you ever seen such a hell on earth?" Fèlicien asked Pierre as they and Thèrese and the ministry men did what little they could for the survivors.

"I pray that this is the worst of it."

It was the worst of it, but it was not the last of the concentration camps.

The commission announced their discovery of Fort Crampel's concentration camp upon their arrival at the next outpost, weakening its administrators' resolve to hide its own camp. At every stop on their route up the Ubangi, the commission claimed a larger number of liberated camps, and the administrators conceded with less resistance.

"I am Commissaire Brazza," Pierre announced as the commission's steamer pulled up to the final outpost. "And I am here to free your slaves."

The trial was held in one of the older administrative buildings, a broad one-story structure that faced a plaza surrounded by smaller administrative buildings and thatched-roof trading posts. More Frenchmen bustled about the plaza that day than Pierre had ever seen assembled in the Congo. There was a crowd of Congolese men and women, too. Some of the Congolese men wore loose cotton shirts and pants and went in bare feet; others were outfitted in linen suits and leather shoes. As the commission approached, the crowd parted. Pierre's name was whispered among them. At Pierre's side was Thérèse, and behind them was Fèlicien, then the nine commissioners of the ministry.

In the crowd was a man named Bankoa, an older Bateke who had lived in the capital for many years under Brazza's administration. He wore a soiled linen coat over a white shirt, gray pants, but no shoes. He had adopted Western attire as a younger man when he learned English and became attached to one of the British firms. He was a liaison to the Congolese who brought rubber and ivory to the trading posts. He had liked his work; he ensured that the Congolese were paid fairly for the goods they collected, and he enjoyed the finest clothing the traders brought into the colony. When Paris removed Brazza and forced out Hatton and Cookson, Bankoa considered joining one of the French firms. But rumblings of forced portage and steep drops in prices kept him away. Instead, he kept to his village and away from the French.

Bankoa's sons were now grown. His shoes had worn through, and he'd not had any new clothes for seven years. He was too old for portage, so it was at great risk that he came to the plaza. But he had to know what would become of the monsters Toquè and Gaud. And here was Brazza!

In Brazza's absence, Bankoa had wished without hope that the Europeans would leave the Congo and the Batekes and their neighbors would know life as it was when he was very young. But the hungry Europeans, he knew, would never leave of their own accord. Bankoa was a pragmatic man. Brazza was the region's best hope; he could restore peace and prosperity for the Congolese—was that not what he and his entourage had come to do?

Beside Brazza and his wife was a young man who was not dressed in the uniform of the nine commissioners and seemed of great importance to Brazza. As the commission awaited the opening of the administrative building's doors and Brazza was conversing with his wife, Bankoa approached the young man.

"You are a friend of Commissaire Brazza?" Bankoa asked.

The young man said he was M. Brazza's secretary. "And his friend," he added.

"Then you are a friend of mine." Bankoa extended his hand, which the man took. "Bankoa."

"Fèlicien."

"You are not from the government, are you?"

"No, I'm a journalist. M. Brazza asked me to help him report on conditions in the colony. Perhaps we can talk later?"

"I can't stay long. I wanted only to see if there would actually be a trial. They won't let us in, though."

"Stick around, and I'll let you know what happens."

"I'll come back tomorrow. I can't stay long." Bankoa's eyes darted around at the administrators. "They'll force me into portage. They're hungry to do it."

"Even an old man like you?"

"Even an old man like me."

"You'd better run along, then. I don't know that the commission can protect you. But you can be sure the forced labor will go in my report."

"Put this in your story," Bankoa whispered. "Every Frenchman here is either a Gaud or a Toquè—a monster who brutalizes or a bureaucrat who acquiesces." He looked for an opening in the perimeter of administrators awaiting entry to the trial, and seeing one, said, "Good day, my friend," to Fèlicien and escaped.

The commission entered the administrative building and was seated in the front row of the gallery. More administrators and curious men from the trading company filed in behind them and took their places. The Congolese remained on the plaza under the watch of administrators posted at the doors.

The gallery was crowded and hot, making for an uncomfortable morning. The judge entered and called for the defendants. Pierre had intended to meet the ministry's counsel, the colonial inspector and lawyer M. Dubard, and the judge before the trial, but the commission had not arrived in Brazzaville in time. It was likely enough that Gentil had instructed them not to meet with him. After what Pierre had seen in the last six weeks, he had little hope that they would be anything but puppets for the commissaire.

An administrator brought Toquè and Gaud into the courtroom. They turned, briefly, toward the gallery; it seemed to Fèlicien that they had been apprised of the commission's presence. Probably by Gentil. They were dressed in clean uniforms. Toquè was thin and expressionless. Certainly, he'd registered the former commissaire's presence, but he didn't let it disturb him, or if it did, he didn't show it. Gaud was stout and smiling; a schoolboy who'd been caught at some mischief. They sat down to hear the charges read.

M. Dubard convinced the judge to permit two Congolese men—men who'd been imprisoned with Papka—to testify. When the first man was brought in, Fèlicien leaned over to Pierre and said, "Perhaps Gentil doesn't have complete control over the trial."

"Gentil risks nothing by allowing Congolese to testify. Toquè and Gaud will deny every word of their testimony."

The prisoners described Toquè shooting a Congolese man for insubordination. "He was very cold. Just shot him without any feeling." Gaud, they said, was the monster who had tied dynamite around Papka's neck. This was done with much feeling. "He enjoyed it."

The ministry had no other witnesses. Pierre said to Fèlicien, "Not a man among them who will cross Gentil."

The defense counsel was a very young man, likely new to the colony. He'd fanned himself with his papers, looking bored, as the prisoners had testified. He did not bother to question them. When the judge called upon him for witnesses, he casually announced that Toquè and Gaud would take the stand.

He questioned Toquè first.

"In your official capacity at Fort Crampel, did you ever execute a man for insubordination or any other reason?"

"Absolutely not."

"Did you witness Fernand Gaud place dynamite on the person of a prisoner?"

"No, I did not."

"Thank you, M. Toquè."

"This is a charade," Pierre said. "Now watch: The ministry's counsel will do nothing."

M. Dubard rose. "M. Toquè. In your pretrial questioning, you claimed that you have, in fact, punished Africans for rebellion and insubordination."

Toquè did not reply.

"Is this correct?" M. Dubard asked.

"Yes."

"Now hold on," Fèlicien said to Pierre. "Perhaps the old man is sympathetic to the Congolese."

"And these punishments have included executions?"

The gathered administrators gasped.

"Yes."

"And in the case of the prisoner Papka, you ordered M. Gaud to execute him?"

"Yes."

"You also stated that to force men into portage, you have ordered subordinates to take women and children as prisoners."

"Yes." More gasps from the gallery. "The commissaire demands porters and entrusts his top administrators to secure them."

"By extortion and threats of death?"

"The commissaire has done nothing but praise my work."

The defense counsel declined to question Gaud. M. Dubard went straight to the trial's heart.

"Did you place dynamite on the prisoner Papka?"

Gaud looked at the defense counsel for guidance.

"Go ahead," the young man said resignedly.

"Yes."

"You believed this would keep the natives in order?"

"Yes. Georges ordered me to kill him."

"That is all, M. Gaud."

With the trial concluded and the commission's report due to Clèmentel by September's end, the commission prepared to return to France. Pierre visited Gentil's office once more; it was his only chance to confront the commissaire following the discovery of the concentration camps and the sentencing of Toquè and Gaud. Pierre was determined to hold nothing back.

While the two commissaires had their tete-a-tete, Thérèse, Fèlicien, and the other commissioners left the Meridien and boarded the steamship. Pierre was to meet them aboard ship, but when he did not arrive at the expected time, Fèlicien and two of the ministry men headed back to the hotel. There they found Pierre slouched in a chair, a clerk patting his forehead with a damp towel.

"Fèlicien," Pierre said, "Where is everyone?"

"Already on board. What's happened?"

"He'd collapsed in the road," the clerk said. "He's feverish."

"I'm all right now."

The two ministry men helped Pierre to his feet.

"Are you sure you ought to get up now?" Fèlicien asked.

"I'm not sure of anything, friend."

"Fèlicien, he needs to be in a hospital."

Thérèse's face was brittle, quaking. Fèlicien had never seen her so frightened. He imagined that she borrowed from her husband's strength; as he had diminished, so had she.

"I'll speak to the captain right away. Go be with him."

The steamship, rather than continue up the Atlantic coast, docked in Dakar. Fèlicien, assisting a shaken Thérèse, solemnly followed two porters as they carried Pierre on a stretcher toward the hospital. As they passed the administrative buildings and trading posts and drew the attention of officers and natives, the ministry men formed a tight circle around Pierre, his porters, and Thérèse and Fèlicien.

The hospital administrator, recognizing the graveness of the French hero's condition, cleared a room. Pierre was attended to briefly by a doctor, the administrator looking nervously upon them. The doctor called Thérèse to him; she was immobile without Fèlicien's help. Fèlicien helped her into a chair opposite the doctor. There was little they could do, the doctor said, only ease his pain. Fèlicien thanked the doctor, who left them with Pierre. Fèlicien found himself with no words for once, so he wiped his spectacles clean for a very long time as he sat next to a broken Thérèse.

"Gentil did this."

"What?"

Before Thérèse could reply, Pierre awakened. His weary and wasted face was breathed new life by his searching eyes. Thérèse drew strength from his eyes, too, and emerged from her slump.

"You're in Dakar, dear."

"Then I was right."

Thérèse wept. Fèlicien squeezed her hand, a proxy for Pierre, then left them alone.

Pierre's thoughts scattered from his weakened mind. He was bled-dry and withered. Where had Fèlicien gone? He had been such a good friend on this, Pierre's final, adventure. Pierre wanted to apologize to him for his brusqueness at the sentencing. He had also been a good friend to Thérèse. Thérèse. Pitiful Thérèse! And little Charles and Antoine and Marthe left with no father!

He ought to tell Thérèse about his meeting with Gentil. And his notes. They must get back to France. He began to speak, and Thérèse took his hand.

When Pierre had visited the commissaire's office again, his dysentery was worsening and making him irritable, and entering Gentil's office, he unleashed his fury unchecked.

"You are a disgrace to France!" he yelled, pointing at the Tricolor hanging behind Gentil's desk. "You are no better than Leopold. And M. Challaye's stories will reveal your abuses to the world."

"Challaye will not be believed."

"*I* will be believed. My own notes will corroborate Fèlicien's stories of your exploitation of the Congolese. Your impossible demands for labor and rubber."

"Come off it—you've forgotten what is required by colonization."

"Torture? Rape? Murder? This is what France demands now?"

"Even you, the friendly colonizer, would not have *liberty, equality, and fraternity* with Blacks."

"Did Gentil give you any food or drink?" Thérèse asked. Pierre did not hear her.

"Remember, Thérèse, my desk-trunk."

"Yes, it's in the steamship's hold."

"Georges Vuitton. Bring him to Clèmentel to open it."

"I will."

"You must tell Fèlicien I am sorry for being short with him the other day."

Toquè and Gaud were sentenced the day after the trial. Pierre, Fèlicien, and the rest of the commission save Therèse, who was resting at the hotel, were present in the gallery with dozens of French administrators. The sentences of five years' imprisonment were met by cries of incredulity by the administrators.

Pierre whispered to Fèlicien, "How do these men not see the justice in this punishment?"

"They are so used to exploiting and abusing Africans, they can't believe the judge would assign Papka's life any value."

Toquè and Gaud, as stoic as they had been throughout the previous day's testimony, were led away. Perhaps, Pierre thought, they don't believe they'll actually have to serve their sentences. The gallery emptied out into the street. Some of the administrators spit upon the Congolese who'd gathered to await news of the sentencing, dispersing them around the corners.

Bankoa, after waiting for the administrators to clear the plaza, approached Fèlicien and said, "Those boys looked very angry."

"Five years' imprisonment for each man," Fèlicien said.

"Five years' imprisonment for each man?"

Fèlicien shook his head in disappointment. "Five years for Papka's life. I'm sorry, my friend, that his life didn't matter more to the judge."

But Bankoa smiled and grabbed Fèlicien's shoulders. "Toquè and Gaud are being imprisoned for five years," he said. He turned to the regrouped Congolese. "Toquè and Gaud are being imprisoned for five years!" he shouted. He shouted it again. Then the Congolese threw their hands up and cheered.

Fèlicien turned back to Pierre. "Imagine their reaction if they were ridding themselves of every Frenchman."

Pierre's eyes narrowed, the warm blue in them hidden. "Are you doubting the colonial mission?"

Fèlicien shrugged. "What I have seen on this adventure does not recommend it."

"You did not see the colony when I was commissaire. What I created was beneficial to France *and* the Congo."

"Yet here we are. I don't envy you the burden of creating this."

Pierre thrust a finger in Fèlicien's face. "I invited you here as a journalist, not a philosopher. Keep in your place!"

Pierre was falling in and out of consciousness. He wasn't sure how much of his stories about Gentil and the sentencing he'd told to Therèse, and how much he'd only recalled to his thoughts.

"You may tell him yourself," Therèse said.

Fèlicien was there. His good friend! "I'm sorry, I had no right to get angry with you the other day. Please forgive me."

Fèlicien searched his memory for when Pierre had been angry with him. After the sentencing? Fèlicien had not forgotten Pierre's words, but their sting had dissipated quickly. The trouble in the colony had devastated Pierre; Fèlicien didn't take his short temper personally.

"Of course I forgive you. Rest now."

Pierre closed his eyes. Fèlicien watched for a long time as Therèse petted Pierre's pathetic face. Pierre's shallow breathing ceased.

Perhaps Fèlicien should have kept his ambivalence to himself. But he had been feeling it since the commission's arrival. The pathos of the concentration camps and the image of Bankoa and the other Congolese celebrating Toquè and Gaud's sentencing were heavy in his thoughts. As was the adjunct thought: Would that the Congolese could throw off their colonizers and truly share in that cherished French ideal—that human ideal: *Liberty, equality, and fraternity.*

PAREIDOLIA

The dead speak from the bedroom box fan. My father's going on about his wish, ultimately unrealized, to retire to an oceanside village. But he never had the do re mi. My brother's telling a funny story about a customer. He didn't actually drown, but we agreed without saying it that he was not waving but drowning. Awakened to my own mortality by their voices, I slip from the bed, careful not to disturb my wife, and go sit on the porch.

The living speak from the wind that's picking up. At the universities, students are toppling statues. For the ones who defend them, my words are inadequate to explain what happens to a dream deferred. At home, we wring our hands over our daughter, who's only in the second grade; so much depends upon a school board meeting!

The not-yet-living speak from the hard rain that starts to batter the earth, the trees, the roof. Our daughter's children. A generation of voices is asking questions about the world ending in fire or ice. I can't understand what any of them is asking, and it's not likely I could give them any satisfactory answers, but I want to know what they're saying.

"Stop," I say, "One at a time."

The door opens.

"Who are you talking to?"

"No one. Everyone."

ACKNOWLEDGMENTS

I'm grateful to several people for helping *The Commission of Inquiry* come together: the Cornerstone Press staff, especially Dr. Ross K. Tangedal, Ellie Atkinson, Chloe Cieszynski, Sophie McPherson, Natalie Reiter, and Ava Willett, for shepherding the book from a manuscript to a Legacy Series title; Scott Miller for the fantastic cover design; Sara Lippman, Ethan Rutherford, and Jennifer Wortman for their lovely blurbs; and Sarah, Lucy, and Will for filling our home with new stories every day.

I'm also grateful to the editors of the following publications, where stories were first published in earlier forms:

"My Father and Ray Gun" in *Gravel*
"Enos" in *Malarkey Books*
"It Is What It Is" in *The Blue Nib*
"Pray for Her" in *Ozone Park Journal* and *Bandit Fiction*
"Dream of the Ambulocetus" in *The River*
"Terminal" in *Door is a Jar*
"Son and Heir" in *Bandit Fiction*
"The Ragpickers at Gettysburg" in *Sundial Magazine*
"Champ" in *Signal Mountain Review*
"Longboxes of Love" in *Queen Mob's Teahouse* and *The Daily Drunk*
"Backhanded Compliments and One-Night Stands" in *me tis*
"Eli's Trouble" in *Jabberwock Review*
"Procession" in *The MacGuffin*
"Mac, Beth" in *Roi Fainéant*
"My Hollywood Story" in *Prick of the Spindle* and *Malarkey Books*
"Pareidolia" in *Free Flash Fiction*

PATRICK NEVINS is the author of *Man in a Cage* (2022). His stories have appeared in *Crab Creek Review, Sundial Magazine, Jabberwock Review, The MacGuffin*, and other journals. He lives with his family in Columbus, Indiana, where he is an associate professor of English.

www.ingramcontent.com/pod-product-compliance
Lightning Source LLC
Chambersburg PA
CBHW061537310726
48972CB00008B/2496